Did she have the courage to ask him?

It made sense to go to the Christmas gala together, she told herself. She was the head of the committee. Cody was in charge of decorations. Who could possibly object?

"Do you have a tux squirreled away someplace?" she asked.

He looked at her, a glint in his eye. "What would be in it for me?"

Paris caught the teasing tone. "Great food. Live band. The oohs and aahs as everyone admires how great you look in a tux."

"You've never seen me in a tux."

She raised a brow. "I have a vivid imagination."

A smile tugged at his lips even as warning bells sounded in his head. He'd give anything to waltz Paris around the dance floor in front of the astonished faces of the town's elite. But could he ever indulge in a dream like that?

She looked him straight in the eye. "So," she challenged, "how about it, Mr. Hawk?"

Books by Glynna Kaye

Love Inspired

Dreaming of Home
Second Chance Courtship
At Home in His Heart
High Country Hearts
Look-Alike Lawman
A Canyon Springs Courtship
Pine Country Cowboy
High Country Holiday

GLYNNA KAYE

treasures memories of growing up in small Midwestern towns—in Iowa, Missouri, Illinois—and vacations spent in another rural community with the Texan side of the family. She traces her love of storytelling to the many times a houseful of great-aunts and great-uncles gathered with her grandma to share hours of what they called "windjammers"—candid, heartwarming, poignant and often humorous tales of their youth and young adulthood.

Glynna now lives in Arizona, and when she isn't writing she's gardening and enjoying photography and the great outdoors.

High Country Holiday

Glynna Kaye

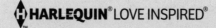

HARLEQUIN® LOVE INSPIRED®

Recycling programs for this product may not exist in your area.

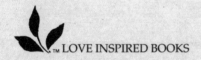 ™ LOVE INSPIRED BOOKS

ISBN-13: 978-0-373-81802-0

High Country Holiday

www.Harlequin.com

Printed in U.S.A.

But the angel said to them, "Do not be afraid. I bring
you good news of great joy that will be for all the
people. Today in the town of David a Savior has
been born to you; He is Christ the Lord."
—*Luke* 2:10–11

For He has rescued us from the dominion of
darkness and brought us into the kingdom of the Son
He loves, in whom we have redemption,
the forgiveness of sins.
—*Colossians* 1:13–14

Forgive as the Lord forgave you.
—*Colossians* 3:13

To Aunt Nancy—
Thank you for being a part of my life.

Chapter One

"Three weddings next month? Are you kidding me?" Paris Perslow cast a look of dismay at the wall calendar in the back room of her father's real estate office on Main Street. The pastor of Canyon Springs Christian Church had to be out of his mind asking her to get involved with this. "December's only a few days away."

Outside the back window, a gust of wind swept snow through the towering ponderosa pines, filling the air with a reminder of the frosty holiday season. While it wasn't by any means the first snowfall of the year in this Arizona mountain community, she wasn't ready for winter.

Or Christmas.

Or Christmas weddings.

Another gust rattled the window, tendrils of cold creeping in around its wooden framework. She stepped away from the glassy panes, thankful for her cashmere sweater.

"My wife would kill me if she knew I was asking you to help." The voice of Pastor Jason Kenton carried over the phone in an apologetic tone. "You know, because…"

Yes, she did know. Because both he and his wife, Reyna, were aware she'd stepped away from responsibilities as a volunteer wedding coordinator when her own dream wedding three and a half years ago had taken a tragic turn.

"I'm sorry about Reyna's illness, Jason, but I don't see how I could pull three weddings together on such short notice." Not if they were anything like the over-the-top extravaganza she and her mother-in-law-to-be had once orchestrated.

"There isn't much left to do," he assured. "Jake Talford and Macy Colston have been planning their wedding since last spring. Sharon and Bill since the summer. And you know the Diaz clan—the whole family will be on top of Abby and Brett's special day. You'd be more of a go-to person representing the church, a reassuring voice for jittery brides and grooms."

Wasn't that *his* job? She paced the hardwood floor, the powerful music of Handel's *Messiah* that emanated from the CD player lending her strength to stand her ground.

"I don't have the time.…"

She'd scheduled church and community-related activities into her calendar months ago, including the Christmas charity gala for which she'd been voted the committee head. Dad, too, had expectations for seasonal entertaining. The holidays, even without a trio of weddings, could be exhausting when you and your widower father played a prominent role in the community.

A pang of apprehension shot through her. Dad wasn't going to like what she intended to tell him after the first of the year…that she'd soon no longer be at his beck and call. That is, if she could garner the courage to make the break. Life away from Canyon Springs? Could she do it?

She had to.

"Would you be willing to think about it?" Jason coaxed. "Maybe pray about it?"

She could almost see his eyebrows rise in question as they often did during Sunday morning messages when challenging his congregation.

"I'm not sure I can commit to doing even that."

"Taking this on may help you work through things," he said gently, again broaching the issue they both knew stood between yes and no. "Weddings are meant to be happy times, Paris. A celebration of God joining two lives for His purposes."

"I understand, but…" While it was difficult seeing others caught up in their happily-ever-afters, the real issue behind her reluctance was one which Pastor Kenton knew nothing about.

"No matter how brides try not to let it get to them," he continued, "the tiniest of setbacks can throw them into a tailspin. But I have confidence you can help these gals keep the right perspective. Honestly, Paris, this shouldn't take much of your time."

A skeptical smile touched her lips. Maybe she'd better get his wife to confirm that. But Reyna hadn't yet been released from the hospital in Show Low, and Jason had mentioned earlier in the conversation that she had a long way to go to recover from a serious bout of pneumonia.

"Could I get back to you tomorrow?" Why was she even saying that? She couldn't allow herself to be sucked into a world of weddings and receptions and starry-eyed couples. Into a world where her "widowed" status drew misunderstanding and undeserved sympathy. But Reyna was more than the pastor's wife, she was a friend.

At her words, Jason perked up. "Tomorrow? You've got it. And no pressure. I promise. Take a look at your calendar and see if you can fit this in."

She knew what the calendar looked like and it wasn't pretty.

"Reyna and I would both be forever in—" He brought himself up short with a self-conscious laugh. "No, no pressure. Think about it. Pray about it. I know this isn't an easy decision to make."

There it was again.

Cody Hawk averted his gaze, pretending not to notice, but it disturbed him just the same. The expression was fleeting, evasive. Sometimes curious, suspicious or even—could he only be imagining it?—silently accusing.

But above all, it was a look of recognition, one that had become annoyingly familiar since returning to his hometown of Canyon Springs two days ago. Not even Christmas melodies piped onto Main Street the morning after Thanksgiving or snowflakes floating through the air made it any more palatable. You'd have thought that after a dozen years people would have forgotten about him and gotten on with their own lives.

Squaring his shoulders, he strode across the street to the office of Perslow Real Estate and Property Management. A two-story natural stone building with a cheery pinecone wreath gracing the door, it exuded a rustic warmth suitable for drawing in newcomers to purchase or rent a piece of what was touted as a mountain country paradise.

Paradise.

The misnomer left a bitter taste in Cody's mouth. The community might be a dream come true for those who had the financial means to buy their way into it, but it showed a much different side to those with lesser resources.

Sleigh bells on the office door announced his entrance, jingling as if delighted to welcome him. Not likely. He closed the door to block a blustery gust, then stuffed his gloves in his pockets, unzipped his jacket and pulled off his baseball cap. A faint tang of pine emanated from a half-decorated Christmas tree in the corner. Several boxes of ornaments and a rope of tinsel lay neglected at its base as if a holiday elf had been suddenly called away.

Although the waiting room was devoid of visitors and no one manned the front desk, he could hear the distinctive strains of Handel's *Messiah* overriding a feminine voice coming from a partially open door. It was a one-sided conversation, as if someone was on the phone.

Had it really been a dozen years since he'd charged out of this place, boiling mad and head held high from having told his father's boss—Paris Perslow's father—what he could do with his job offer?

Dumb kid. He hadn't been old enough or smart enough to know burning bridges could come back to haunt you. What was that parting line he'd tossed at Mr. Perslow that memorable afternoon? *Just you wait and see. Someday you'll be groveling at my feet. Sir.*

Cody groaned inwardly at the sarcasm with which he'd laced that final word of his tirade. Well, he might be only minutes away from being shown the door, but what choice did he have?

Reluctantly moving to the seating area, he'd barely lowered himself into a burgundy leather chair when the final notes of the classic Christmas choral piece faded away as the woman in the back room wrapped up the conversation. Her lilting tones now clearly reached Cody's ears.

A viselike sensation tightened around his chest.

It couldn't be, could it? But that voice…

He stood and moved swiftly to the door. This wasn't the time or place for a reunion. Not when anyone could walk in on them at any minute. Her dad. A coworker. *Her husband.*

"May I help you?" a melodious voice called from behind him as he reached for the doorknob.

He tensed, willing his heart to slide down out of his throat and back into his chest. *Please let this be a cousin. A long-lost sister.* With effort, he turned to look directly into the smoky-gray eyes of a woman far more exquisite than the girl he'd long remembered.

A soft charcoal sweater, jeans, English riding-style boots and dark brown hair pulled loosely into a low ponytail gave her the carefully casual appearance of an American aristocrat. High cheekbones touched by a whisper of rose and delicately arched eyebrows underlined the air of seemingly flawless refinement.

But he knew the satiny gloss on a too-tempting mouth camouflaged a scar acquired in third grade. She'd been running from playground bullies, slipped on a graveled walkway and cut her lower lip. He remembered the day well, his first at the new school as a fifth grader. He'd retaliated on her behalf by bloodying a few noses, got sent home…and forever lost his heart to Paris Perslow.

Or rather, Paris Herrington.

Mrs. Dalton Jenner Herrington III.

* * *

Heart pounding, Paris stared up at the boy she'd known since grade school. A man now. Tall. Muscular. Rugged. A shock of raven hair slashed across his forehead and the high cheekbones gave credence to talk of Native American blood in his ancestry. Sharp, black-brown eyes pierced into hers.

"Remember me, Paris?" His words, tinged with the faintest of Texas accents, held a note of self-deprecating humor as he no doubt recalled their last meeting.

How could she forget him? Not only had he been her self-appointed guardian from third grade onward, raising the ire of teachers, classmates and her father alike, but her last encounter with him had left her more than shaken.

"I'm sorry to hear of your father's stroke, Cody."

His jaw, graced with a five o'clock shadow even this early in the morning, hardened. "Bad situation."

"Is he… Has there been any improvement?"

A humorless smile touched Cody's lips. "He still can't talk much. I'd say that's an overall improvement, wouldn't you?"

Paris flinched at the candid judgment. While the burly Leroy Hawk could be a charmer when he chose to be, his humor was sometimes biting and unforgiving. She'd often wondered why her father kept him on as an employee.

Clearly, though, there was still no love lost between father and son despite over a decade's separation. Which wasn't surprising. In elementary school, Cody had once furtively raised his ragged T-shirt to show her the ugly bruises—but only after he'd made her promise never to tell.

She hadn't told.

But she should have.

Ignoring Cody's harsh question, she restlessly moved to the Christmas tree and picked up a box of glass ornaments. "How is your mother holding up?"

Cody had adored Lucy Hawk, and Paris suspected that as a kid he'd deliberately drawn his father's anger in an effort to protect her from the short-tempered man's fists.

"Working too hard."

She always had, and now Leroy's health setback would make it even harder on her. Paris removed an ornament from the box and hooked a metal hanger into its loop. "I bought the wreath on the door from Dix's. It's one of hers. Canyon Springs is fortunate to have her working on the annual Christmas gala this year. She's a true craftsman—a gifted artist."

"I'll let Ma know you think so."

For several moments, neither of them spoke. What more was there to say that *could* be said? A tremor of awareness skittered as Cody's dark eyes remained fixed on her, and she self-consciously hung the ornament on the tree. He'd always looked at her that way. It was in many ways the same look other men had long been known to give her—appreciative of her beauty. But with Cody there had been something else. A tenderness. An almost…reverence.

That had always been her undoing, and she'd long guarded against it. Abruptly she turned toward him. "I'm sorry, is there something I can help you with?"

He cleared his throat. "I'm here to see your father."

Regarding Leroy's job security? His insurance? His stroke wasn't workers'-compensation-related. Everyone in town knew he'd blown last Friday's paycheck on lottery tickets and booze, then when the multimillion-dollar winning number was drawn—and it wasn't his—he'd suffered a stroke.

Her own father had seemed more agitated about the whole thing than she would have expected. Had he anticipated this visit from Cody, asking special favors for his father, maybe applying legal pressure?

"I'm afraid Dad left for the Valley this morning. He'll be gone for a few days. Remember, this *is* a holiday weekend."

Cody's brows lowered.

"He left you here to watch over things?" His glance raked the office, then focused again on her. "All alone?"

Gazing up at the big man, a ripple of unease skimmed her spine. But that kind of thinking was preposterous. Cody might look menacing, but he'd never so much as attempted to lay a hand on her during the years she'd known him. Not even that last day when he'd stepped out of the darkness and frightened her half out of her wits with his crazy talk.

Nevertheless…

"Everett's here. And Kyle. Or at least they'll be back in few minutes." She moved behind the receptionist's desk, placing a barrier between them. She didn't know Cody now. She hadn't really known him back then, either. And although he'd never crossed any lines with her, he *was* a Hawk.

"I don't," he stated, "have business with Everett or Kyle."

"Perhaps there's something I can—"

"I need to see your father."

"I'd be happy to schedule an appointment for Monday." She did her best to keep her tone cheerful despite his terse responses. She'd warn her dad, of course, so he wouldn't be caught unprepared.

Cody exhaled a resigned breath. "First thing Monday morning then."

She opened the scheduling software program. "Nine-thirty?"

"There's nothing earlier?"

You'd have thought she'd suggested high noon. He'd been an early riser as a kid, with chores to see to before he came to school. Maybe old habits died hard?

"Dad often works late in the evening with clients, so yes, nine-thirty is customary."

"Fine."

He didn't sound as though it were fine, but she typed his name into the database. "May I let him know what the appointment concerns?"

"He'll know."

Did he have to sound so confrontational? That wouldn't go over well with Dad. It didn't go over well with her, either. Cody might never have had much patience with those in authority, but he'd always been more than polite with her.

As if coming to the same realization, he nodded toward the computer, his tone softening. "I mean, he'll know I'm here about my father's situation. I need to find out where things stand regarding his employment status and medical benefits."

She nodded and made the note. When she glanced up, he was watching her with that look that had been typical of Cody since the first day she'd met him. Self-consciously she ran her tongue along her lower lip. Across the scar.

"Well, you're all set," she said with a businesslike clip to her words. "Nine-thirty on Monday morning."

"Thank you." He placed his ball cap on his head, zipped his jacket and started to turn away. Then he paused to look down at her once again. "So you're filling in here while visiting Canyon Springs over the Thanksgiving holiday?"

"I live here. I'm a real estate agent."

His expression darkened slightly.

"Was there something else?" She held her breath, the pulse in her throat racing as his gaze lingered, indecision flickering through his eyes.

"No." He shook his head. "Have a good rest of your day, Paris."

And then he was gone, the sleigh bells chiming a farewell as the door closed behind him.

Exhaling, she leaned back in the chair and closed her eyes.

Cody Hawk had returned to town.

But he wouldn't be here for long. He'd made that clear. He had family business to take care of, then would disappear into the night as he'd done a dozen years ago. Thankfully, he hadn't attempted to express condolences for the death of her fiancé. Nor had he made reference to their last meeting.

When he'd confessed he loved her.

She'd been certain he intended to kiss her that night and, to her shame, she'd wanted him to. But when she'd come to her senses and rejected the outpouring of his heart—as her father would have expected of her—he'd had the audacity to claim that one day he'd return to town and she'd beg him to marry her.

She hurried to the windows to peek between the wooden-louvered slats at a departing Cody. Collar turned up against the wind-driven snow and hands rammed in his jacket pockets, he crossed the street with that same mesmerizing, masculine grace he'd grown into as a teen. He'd been all male from adolescence onward and even the nice girls noticed. But while a nice girl might dream a dangerous dream, in a little town like this she wouldn't dare throw away her—and her family's—reputation for a boy with kin like Cody's.

Paris herself had been more than aware of him those many years ago, aware of his slow, lazy smile and barely-under-the-surface interest evidenced in the way he looked at her. That look had both excited and frightened her youthful heart, for he was a Hawk. Forbidden territory for a Perslow.

She abruptly stepped back from the window, irritated at herself for gawking after the still-enticing man. She was twenty-eight years old now. He was what—thirty? He'd been living his life elsewhere, doing who knew what, far from the vigilant eyes of Canyon Springs. He'd probably been up to no good, just like his father and older half brothers. Dad always said even a shiny apple didn't fall far from the tree.

But that didn't mean it wasn't tempting.

She returned to the Christmas tree where she picked up another ornament. She wasn't a teenager now, given to indulging in silly daydreams. Cody would soon be gone and his return to Canyon Springs a mere blip on the radar of her life.

With an air of resolve, she slipped a hook into the ornament loop and placed it on the end of a branch.

But before she could react, the too-fragile needles bent, sending the decorative glass ball tumbling to the hardwood floor where it shattered at her feet.

Chapter Two

Cody strode to the old Dodge pickup, jerked open the door and climbed inside. Then he slammed the door and sat staring blindly out the snow-streaked windshield.

It was clear Paris couldn't wait to send him on his way. He couldn't blame her. How old had she been back then—almost sixteen? He'd been nearly eighteen and old enough to know better than to do what he'd done that night. He could still hear her soft gasp when he'd stepped out of the shadows where she'd been relaxing on the porch swing. He'd been desperate to speak to her before he left town, daring to risk being caught by her father.

Looking back, he was lucky she hadn't called the cops.

And yet…for a fleeting moment, he thought he'd seen something in her eyes that sustained him with a glimmer of hope despite her firm but gentle turndown. It kept him going as he endeavored to turn his life around and become a man worthy of a woman like Paris. That is, until the day four years ago when he'd come across her engagement announcement on the front page of the online local paper.

Yeah, he'd been a dumb kid in more ways than one. He wasn't that bright of an adult, either. He hadn't spoken to Paris in twelve and a half years, yet he'd neglected to say it was good to see her. He hadn't told her how beautiful she was. Nor could he bring himself to offer congratulations on her marriage into the Herrington clan.

Dalton Herrington.

Cody's fists clenched involuntarily at the thought of the hotshot physician marrying Paris. But with Dalton's professional status and upper-crust social standing in the community, he was exactly the kind of man she'd have been expected to marry. No surprises there. The future doctor had been in the same graduating class as Cody, likely finishing up medical school and heading into a residency program three and a half years ago. But even though he hadn't been one to give Cody grief like others in the popular crowd, Cody didn't want to think about them being a married couple who'd probably soon be starting a family of little high-class Herringtons.

For all he knew, they already had.

"Cody!" A sharp rapping at the driver-side window startled him back to the present.

He turned to find an auburn-haired, fifty-something woman smiling at him and his spirits lifted as he stepped out to join her. Sharon Dixon, owner of Dix's Woodland Warehouse, had always been good to his mom. To him, too, come to think of it. Funny how you forgot things like that.

The once-robust woman had lost considerable weight, though, since he'd last seen her. Had she been ill? His mother hadn't mentioned it but, then again, after Paris's engagement he no longer checked online to see what the pretty Miss Perslow might be up to, and forbade Ma to share any Canyon Springs gossip with him.

"As I live and breathe," Sharon whispered, her former smoker's voice as rough as sandpaper. "I'd heard you were back in town, doll. I'm sure your mother is tickled to pieces."

He noticed she didn't include his dad in that observation.

"Look at you. All grown up." Her smile widened as she took him in from his booted toes to the baseball cap on his head. "I imagine you're beating off the girls with a bat these days."

He gave a dubious chuckle. "I can't say that's been much of a problem."

"It will be if you stick around here for long." She winked.

Right. While women elsewhere didn't seem to have any objections to what reflected back at him in his mirror, he doubted any in this town would line up to compete for a guy who'd grown up on the wrong side of the tracks.

"I'm glad our paths crossed today, Cody. I have something for you to give your mom." She dipped her fingers into a jacket pocket, then handed him a check. "It's payment for wreaths and table decorations she left on consignment last week. They sold out within days."

He glanced at the amount on Dix's Woodland Warehouse check stock, then raised a brow. He used to gather bags of ponderosa pinecones for Ma, but had no idea people paid that kind of money for homemade Christmas decorations. He pulled out his wallet and tucked the check inside. "I'll see she gets this."

When she wasn't with Dad.

"I've hesitated to contact her with all that's going on." Sharon gazed at him with sympathy. "But I have customers asking about future deliveries. There would be guaranteed sales if she can find time to put together more wreaths. The greenery or pinecone variety both sell well. Those quilted table runners are popular, too."

"Thanks. I'll let her know, Mrs. Dixon."

"It's Sharon." She wagged a finger at him. "I thought we went through this when you were a teenager."

They had, but he still felt funny calling her by her first name. His Texas-born mama had been a stickler for proper etiquette, Mister and Missus being drilled into him from infancy. Not that his manners had made any difference in this town.

"I'll give the message to her...Sharon."

She studied him for a long moment, windblown snowflakes lighting in her hair. "How is your father?"

Not many asked. Not many cared. But he knew Sharon's concern, like Paris's, was genuine, not merely fishing for gossip to share with neighbors who clucked their tongues at those no-good Hawk men. Dad couldn't care less about their disapproval, but Cody knew it hurt Ma, even though she'd never said as much.

"He's as well as can be expected." Which meant Leroy Hawk wasn't happy and was making sure no one else was, either. The wind shifted direction, whipping around them with a blustery gust. "You'd better get back inside, ma'am, before this wind knocks you off your feet."

"Tell your mother she's in my prayers. You are, too."

"Thanks." He'd willingly take any prayers he could get, for within hours of crossing the Canyon Springs city limits, anger and resentments he thought God had put to rest resurfaced. And now, finding Paris living here... He hadn't expected the ambitious Dalton Herrington to settle down as a small-town doctor.

For a moment he thought Sharon might try to hug him, but apparently his expression prevented that. Instead, she fixed a look on him that said she understood more than he gave her credit for, then she headed back to her store.

Mrs. Dixon had always gone out of her way for his mother, for which he was grateful. It still galled, though, to know people were aware of your lack. That people—like Paris—knew you and yours were struggling and in need of a handout.

But, God willing, not much longer.

"Oh, sweetheart, this dress is breathtaking on you." Saturday morning, the well-coiffed Elizabeth Herrington stepped back to better view Paris in the three-way mirror outside the dressing rooms of a Canyon Springs boutique. "If only Dalton were here to see you."

Paris stiffened, avoiding Elizabeth's misty-eyed gaze in the reflection before her.

"I don't know…" She swished the skirt from side to side, the exhilaration she'd felt when she'd slipped into the floor-length gown evaporating at the mention of Dalton's name.

She didn't fault Elizabeth, though. Widowed not long before the loss of Dalton, she'd loved her only son dearly and generously included Paris in that all-embracing affection. Right from the beginning, when her mother died when Paris was fourteen, Elizabeth had stepped into her best friend's shoes to comfort and guide, to treat Marna and Merle Perslow's daughter as if she were her own. What could possibly have been more natural, more gratifying for her efforts, than to have the girl she adored grow up to marry her only son?

But Elizabeth's fondness had been undeserved. She had no idea Dalton would still be alive...if it hadn't been for Paris.

"I'll think about it." She turned her back to the sales associate to be unzipped.

Elizabeth frowned her disappointment. "It's only a few weeks until the charity event. In this dress you'll be the belle of the ball. It fits as if made for you, and the black velvet sets off your dark hair and fair complexion to perfection."

That's what Paris had thought, too. At first, anyway. Now the dress had lost its luster.

"Please hold this until you hear from me," Elizabeth instructed the sales associate, not questioning that her instructions would be followed even if it might cost the boutique a sale. There were certain advantages to being a Herrington in this town.

Paris returned to the dressing room to change into her street clothes. As much as she loved Elizabeth, as good as Dalton's mom had always been to her, would the dear woman ever let her live her life outside the confines of a relationship with her son?

Maybe this shadow world was Paris's penalty for having attempted to go against family wishes three and a half years ago. Which made what she planned to do now—leave Canyon Springs—seem all the more disloyal to those who loved her.

Once outside the shop, Elizabeth motioned her toward Dix's Woodland Warehouse. "Let's take a look at Dix's seasonal items. I love how it's decorated this year. I think Sharon's daughter has played a huge part in that."

Newly married Kara Kenton was an interior designer, a local girl who'd escaped for a time to Chicago and made her mark on the world. Paris didn't even know where she herself would start if given such an opportunity. She had many interests. Events planning. Gourmet cooking. Photography. Her unfinished degree was in elementary education. How could she choose?

Unlike yesterday, this morning the sun shone in a brilliant blue sky. Although still chilly, the wind had abated and Paris had donned a fitted wool blazer rather than a heavier jacket. Such crazy, patchwork weather in mountain country.

"Isn't this wreath beautiful?" Elizabeth stopped to admire the door decoration as they stepped up onto the porch at Dix's. "It would be perfect in my foyer, don't you think?"

"If it's not for sale, I imagine you can commission one from Lucy Hawk."

"That poor woman, being married to that lowlife Leroy." Elizabeth discreetly lowered her voice as she held open the door to the store. "He got what he had coming, but it will make life more difficult for her. Those sons of his haven't lifted a finger to help, either. They should be ashamed of themselves."

Paris bit back the impulse to defend Leroy's youngest. But she couldn't speak to what Cody's intentions were. Taking sides with a Hawk—any Hawk—wouldn't be advisable.

Once inside the store, they greeted proprietor Sharon Dixon who was dressed in a Christmas-themed sweatshirt, her head topped with a jaunty Santa Claus hat. Then they moved eagerly through the store to take in the abundance of Christmas wares mixed with the usual outdoor gear and general-store staples.

While Elizabeth wandered off, Paris moved to the Christmas tree in the center of the raftered room where tiny fairy lights and dozens of hand-made ornaments were arranged in a heartwarming display. She had a collection of mountain-themed decorations and, as always, was eager to add one more. This year's selection would be particularly special for her as, if all went as hoped, it would be her last as a resident of Canyon Springs.

"Parker will be in town for the holidays," Elizabeth pointed out when she eventually rejoined Paris, her arms laden with Christmas merchandise.

"That's nice." Paris avoided her gaze. Dad had also mentioned Dalton's cousin Parker a time or two in recent weeks, expressing pleasure that the up-and-coming attorney might return to Canyon Springs to partner in the same law firm with city councilman Jake Talford.

As if this town needed another lawyer.

But Paris wasn't interested in being railroaded into a relationship with Parker Herrington.

"You *are* going to need an escort for the Christmas gala, you know."

"Actually," Paris said, "as the head of the committee this year, I'll be behind the scenes more often than not, seeing to details of the event. I don't want to be tied to someone with the expectation that I keep them entertained."

Her best friend would be home soon and, as far as she knew, didn't have a date for the gala, either. Maybe they could hang out together. As always, the high-spirited Delaney Marks would pitch in on anything that needed doing—like keeping Paris sane.

Elizabeth pursed her lips. "Parker is capable of entertaining himself and would be a strong complement to your talent for hosting social events such as this."

"Elizabeth, I—"

"Ho ho ho!" a low, masculine voice called from the front door. "Look what I found, Sharon. Ma had a stash of finished ones out in the shed. There's more in my truck."

Startled, Paris turned to see Cody making his way to the checkout counter, his arms laden with beribboned wreaths. Hope sparked. If she could ditch Dalton's mother, maybe now would be an ideal opportunity to talk to him regarding a unsettling phone call she'd received earlier that morning about his mother's role in the Christmas gala.

Considering the nature of that untimely call from a committee member, she should never have given in last night to what she thought was God nudging her to contact Pastor Kenton and agree to take on the weddings.

Elizabeth raised a brow disdainfully as she lowered her voice to a whisper. "Isn't that one of those Hawk boys?"

"Maybe he's here to help his parents."

Elizabeth sniffed. "That'll be the day."

Sharon clapped her hands in delight. "Lucy had these made up? Why didn't she bring them in? Customers are begging for more."

"I imagine she intended to, but with everything that's happened in the past week…" He shrugged, then motioned to the wreaths he'd placed on the counter. "Being kept in the cold shed, they still look and smell as fresh as you could hope for."

"They do look nice. I'll get busy calling people on the waiting list." Still smiling, Sharon placed her hands on her hips and looked up at him. "Aren't you the finest of Santa's helpers, doll."

With a laugh, she impulsively whipped off her holiday hat and stood on tiptoe to secure it on Cody's handsome head. Startled, he glanced uneasily around the store, no doubt to ensure no one had observed the indignity of his impromptu elf act.

Paris couldn't help but smile, but she didn't anticipate the knee-buckling impact when his dark-eyed gaze collided with hers.

Chapter Three

Cody groaned inwardly. Not because Paris caught him with the silly hat on his head, but because she was more beautiful today than she'd been yesterday. How was that even possible?

He swallowed the lump forming in his throat as the seconds ticked, taking in her trim, shapely figure, the brightness of her expressive gray eyes, the delicate curve of her sweet mouth…

Then, coming to his senses, he broke eye contact when he realized she wasn't alone. A frowning Elizabeth Herrington stood beside her. Her mother-in-law.

He sheepishly removed the ridiculous hat from his head, then handed it to Sharon. "I'll get the rest of the wreaths out of the truck."

"Do that, doll. I'll move these to a back room. It's warm in here with that woodstove blazing away."

He nodded, his eyes averted from Paris, then headed outside. He let down the tailgate and lifted the lightweight tarp to reveal half a dozen more wreaths. Well, it could have been worse. It could have been Paris's husband who caught him staring awestruck at his beautiful wife. Her mother-in-law catching him in the act was bad enough.

Mrs. Herrington was no doubt aware that Merle Perslow had warned him off more than once as a teenager and that a stipulation of that job offer twelve years ago included keeping his distance from his daughter. That's what had set off Cody's temper that day. That and the man's patronizing air that he was doing the community a favor by hiring the son of Leroy Hawk to keep him off the streets and out of trouble.

He didn't have long to wait until, from the corner of his eye, he caught a package-laden Mrs. Herrington and Paris exiting the store. Deep in conversation, the older woman didn't glance in his direction, but Paris clearly spied him, then quickly looked away.

Counting slowly to one hundred to ensure they'd walked down the shop-lined street, he'd no sooner lifted the remaining wreaths into his arms when he saw Paris heading briskly back in his direction.

"Good morning, Cody." Her voice came somewhat breathlessly when she halted before him.

"Paris." He nodded an acknowledgment as he placed the wreaths back in the truck bed, his heart beating faster at this unexpected chance to speak with her.

"I'm sorry to bother you, but I got a call earlier this morning about your mother."

He frowned. "My ma? Is something wrong?"

"I'm hoping not." She clasped her gloved hands in front of her, her expression troubled. "It has to do with the annual Christmas gala. I'm the committee head this year."

He was more than familiar with the event, but managed not to grimace. It was a charity dinner and dance that had been a community tradition since long before Cody's family had moved to Canyon Springs. It was for a good cause, of course. But he'd been mortified more than once when his father insisted he line up with other underprivileged children to receive a token toy or item of winter clothing as society's elite looked on benevolently, proud as peacocks of their generosity toward the community's needy.

Needy. It was all he could do to keep his lip from curling at a word reminiscent of a poor Dickensian urchin timidly holding out a bowl for cold porridge. How he despised the image.

He cleared his throat. "You'd mentioned yesterday that my mother is helping. She's making a few decorations, right?"

"More than a few, I'm afraid." A tiny crease formed between Paris's brows. "Some on the committee are concerned that, with your father's illness demanding so much of her time, she won't be able to fulfill her obligations."

"Exactly how many decorations has she agreed to make?" Dad might not always make good on promises, but no one would ever accuse his mother of that. Maybe, though, he should have asked permission before carting off to Dix's the stash of wreaths he'd found in the shed? He'd thought he was doing her a favor.

Paris slipped her hands into her jacket pockets. "Unfortunately, it's more than that. She's overseeing the decorating this year. The props. Christmas trees. Centerpieces. The works."

He gave a low whistle. "I'm surprised she took that on, but I doubt she'll be able to do it now. She's at the hospital almost around the clock and there's no telling how long Dad will be there. I suggest you look elsewhere for a volunteer."

"That's just it. She *isn't* a volunteer." Paris hesitated, as if reluctant to continue. "She's been contracted for a design she submitted several months ago, and she received payment in advance for her time and materials."

Cody flinched. He hadn't expected that. His mother must have needed the money badly. Why hadn't she told him?

"I can reimburse the committee, Paris. That's no problem."

Or it wouldn't be if things worked out as he and his business partner hoped.

Paris offered a feeble smile. "That's thoughtful of you, but the gala is three weeks from tonight, and I've been told nothing at the staging site has been touched in over a week. There's always a last-minute scramble, but usually by this time things are coming together. A few committee members are concerned that she intended to have your father build the sets. And now…"

Leroy Hawk volunteered to do something of that nature? No way. Ma must have had another plan.

"If I reimburse the committee, can't you get someone else to take over?"

A flicker of irritation lit her eyes. "I'll certainly do my best if it comes to that. I know I should talk to your mother directly, but when I saw you here…"

With Dad's situation demanding her every waking moment, Ma probably lost track of time. But he could tell this turn of events had unsettled Paris. The charity event was a huge responsibility on those young, slender shoulders.

"Let me talk to her. And don't worry about it, okay?" He met Paris's gaze with a firm one intended to reassure. "I imagine she has everything under control, but hasn't had time to update the committee."

"Thank you." She tilted her head, the expression in her eyes conveying her gratitude—and reminiscent of the look she'd given him the day long ago when he'd flown to her aid on the playground. "Your mother has my cell phone number, but I can give it to you, too, so you can get in touch with me."

He pulled out his phone and punched in the

numbers she recited, then gave her his. But as he watched her head off down the street, he knew this exchange would be far sweeter if she wasn't married to Dalton Herrington.

Back inside Dix's, Sharon motioned for him to follow her to the rear of the store with his armload of wreaths. "I thought you'd fallen down a hole or something."

"No, no holes." Except for the gaping one in his heart.

Inside the storeroom, Sharon took one of the wreaths and placed it on an empty shelf. "How long will you be in town?"

"I'm not sure." He handed her another wreath. "Dad's situation is uncertain and I can't talk to his boss until Monday. But there's plenty to keep me busy at my folks' place in the meantime. Ma hadn't said a word about it, but Dad's let things go since I left."

"You know that I still check on her, don't you? I make sure she's doing all right."

"It's good to know there are people I can count on to make sure Dad doesn't get out of line." Cody grimaced. "Pastor Kenton does the same. Ma and I communicate through occasional phone calls he arranges at the church office. It's better for Ma that Dad not be aware of that."

"I figured you'd keep in touch with her. While life isn't easy being married to your father, I feel certain Lucy hasn't come to any physical harm. God's kept watch."

"He has. But He's had help from the sidelines, as well." Cody placed the last wreath on a shelf. Confession time. "This isn't something I'm proud of, but the night before I left town I told him if he ever laid a hand on Ma, I'd find out about it…and come back to kill him."

Startled eyes rose to his.

He met her gaze without blinking. "I meant it, too, and he knew it."

Sharon offered a dry smile. "It sounds as if I have more to thank the good Lord for in regard to Lucy's safekeeping—and your father's—than I originally thought I did."

"Amen." Cody cracked a smile of his own. "And I don't use that word lightly."

She tilted her head in question.

"It's a long story, but suffice it to say that my name is now recorded in God's Book of Life."

"Well, I'll be." Before he could stop her, she reached up to loop her arms around his neck and pulled him down for a quick hug. "Happiest day of your mother's life."

"And my old man's luckiest."

Sharon chuckled. "You've always been a good boy, Cody. Deep down, I mean. You had some rocky years and I know things were rough what with your father and those two brothers of yours setting the stage. This may never be a place you want to call home, but I know your mother's thrilled you're here now to help out however you can."

He ducked his head. He wasn't worthy of Sharon's praise. He wasn't in town because he wanted to be but because that scripture he'd come across last weekend had punched him in the gut. *Anyone who does not provide for their relatives, and especially for their own household, has denied the faith.*

Yeah, he'd seen to Ma's needs as much as he could, as much as she'd let him. But God had impressed on him to be here as His representative in the flesh this time.

"Well, I'd better get going. There's lots of work to be done at their place." He needed to find out what was up with Ma and the charity event, too.

"You *are* a regular Christmas elf, aren't you?"

"That's me." But they both knew this had never been his favorite season. It always brought too many reminders that he wasn't as well-off as the other kids in town. Too many humiliating opportunities for his dad to send him around for handouts.

Sharon gave him an apologetic glance. "I'm sorry if I embarrassed you in front of Paris and Elizabeth with this silly hat." She waggled her head to send the puffy white ball swinging.

He laughed and snatched it off her head, then popped it on top of his. "No problem. I'm sure I'm the most handsome elf this town has ever seen."

"I imagine you're the most handsome one *Paris* has ever seen."

"I don't know about that." He handed the hat back to her. "I imagine her husband can hold his own—if supplied appropriate headgear, of course."

Sharon's forehead creased. "Her husband?"

"Dalton." Why was she looking at him as if he'd lost his mind? "Dr. Dalton Herrington?"

"You *have* been gone a long time, doll." She placed a gentle hand on his arm. "Paris never married Dalton. He died. Didn't you know?"

"A tuck here and there and it will be a perfect fit," Paris reassured Macy Colston late Saturday afternoon as they exited the Sew-In-Love shop where the final fitting of the young woman's bridal dress had taken place. Low, slate-gray clouds once again hinted at a possibility of snow, the Northland's weather changeable from one minute to the next.

"Thanks again, Paris, for stepping in to take over for Reyna. With all the traveling for my *Hometowns With Heart* blog and my family scattered across the country, I've probably depended on her more than I should. Hopefully I won't infringe on your time too much."

Paris patted the leather portfolio tucked under her arm. "Thankfully, Reyna is extremely organized. Your wedding will be utterly charming with the 1940s theme. I love that Jake's agreeing to wear a fedora and has a friend with a vintage car. So dashing—and romantic."

"He's being a real sport. You have no idea the

lengths a man in love will—" Macy brought herself up short, an apologetic look darkening her eyes. "I'm sorry, Paris. Of course you know. Hearing women babble on about their fiancés and weddings can't be easy. Please forgive me if I've been insensitive."

Paris shook her head, determined not to allow a stab of guilt to affect her response. "I love your excitement at God's gift of marriage. That is in no way being insensitive to what happened to me."

When she and Macy parted, Paris headed to her SUV where she paused to leave a phone message for Abby Diaz, suggesting a time for a face-to-face meeting. She'd already spoken with Sharon and hopefully assisting the two of them would be no more time-consuming than Macy and Jake's wedding appeared to be.

With the strong possibility that she might be compelled to dive into decorating for the Christmas gala, she'd need every spare minute she could get. She should have foreseen that this could happen when she'd first heard of Leroy's setback, and not agreed to take on the weddings.

She glanced at her watch. Cody hadn't called yet. Had he forgotten he'd promised to talk to his mother? Should she call to remind him? No. That sounded teenager-ish, as if she wanted an excuse to talk to him.

But what she could do in the meantime was drive out to Pine Shadow Ridge, a gated community which Perslow Property Management oversaw. Its impressive clubhouse would once again be the site of the Christmas charity event. She could confirm that there was no sign of Lucy Hawk's recent decorating activity. In fact, she *should* have confirmed it before speaking with Cody. What if that committee member was wrong? Sharlene Odel often thrived on conflict. What if things were right on schedule and Lucy took offense at Paris not trusting her?

Not far outside the city limits, Paris slowed to take a sharp turn before heading up a blacktopped, tree-lined lane. Ahead she spotted the stone gatehouse and the security gate where an older-model pickup nosed up to the wrought-iron barrier. The gatekeeper had stepped out of his shelter, shaking his head and motioning for the driver to back up. Harry Campbell knew all the residents and vendors authorized to come and go. Apparently this one didn't pass muster.

Allowing adequate space for the truck to back up, Paris put the SUV in Park, adjusted the heater and settled in to wait. Hopefully Harry would get this straightened out quickly and she could be on her way.

But…wait. Wasn't that truck similar to the one Cody had been driving? Turning off the ignition, Paris stepped out into the nippy late-afternoon air. A few snowflakes kissed her cheeks as she approached the gatehouse, and Harry's polite but firm voice reached her ears.

"I'm sorry, sir, but like I said, you have to move. You're blocking those who are authorized for entrance." Harry glanced in her direction, then motioned apologetically toward the truck. "Sorry, Miss Perslow."

At the mention of her name, Cody poked his handsome head out the driver-side window to look back in her direction.

"Paris, please tell this guy I'm legit. Like I told him, I'm here on behalf of the Christmas gala."

Did he intend to personally check out the status of his mother's work, to see how bad it was—or wasn't?

"He's legit," she confirmed as she came to stand by the irritated gatekeeper. Then she cast a cool glance toward Cody, who flashed an I-told-you-so look in Harry's direction. "It's customary, Mr. Hawk, to have authorization in advance. Harry wouldn't be doing his job had he let you in."

No doubt Harry had taken one look at Cody's weathered vehicle and decided this man had no business there. He'd know Leroy, of course, and could easily have gone to school with one of Cody's troublemaking brothers. A Hawk was a Hawk in this town, with a one-size-fits-all reputation.

She nodded to the gatekeeper. "Thanks, Harry. I'll vouch for him."

But was that wise? She had to keep reminding herself that Cody might have been a much-maligned boy who'd always been kind to her, but she had no idea who he was as a man.

Harry nodded and returned to the gatehouse, then the massive gates slowly opened. She glanced at Cody.

"Do you know where you're going?"

He shook his head and grinned, a heart-stopping flash of white teeth in his tanned face. "Why don't you lead the way, Miss Perslow?"

Back in her SUV, endeavoring to quiet the now-skittering beat of her heart, she watched Cody ease his truck through the gate. Then she followed until he pulled over to let her pass. The tree-lined lane curved among pines and boulders, a gradual incline that wouldn't give anyone too much wintertime grief. The majority of residents vacated after Labor Day, of course, not returning until early summer. But diehards remained throughout the year or returned on winter weekends to ski nearby slopes and cozy up to a roaring fireplace.

When they reached the top of the rise, the log-and-stone clubhouse came into distant view through the pines, but she took a sharp right turn down a narrow blacktopped road marked "Private." When she finally reached the large steel structure where heavy maintenance equipment and supplies were housed, she shut off the engine and got out as Cody pulled in beside her.

As he approached where she stood next to the

substantial building, his dark eyes assessed his surroundings.

"This is new. And I'm guessing that was the clubhouse I glimpsed before we turned off. The foundation was being poured about the time I left town."

She'd forgotten he'd have still lived in Canyon Springs when the project was getting underway. Motioning to a door off to the side, she held a key-card to the security pad next to it. Cody reached for the latch and opened it for her.

"Thanks," she said as she stepped into the dimly lit interior, noting that the workers had left for the day. She felt along the wall for the light switch just as Cody reached for it, too, his warm fingers brushing hers as together they illuminated the high-ceilinged space. She pulled back as a shot of awareness bolted through her.

Catching her breath, she pointed across the spacious interior to the far corner. "We've set up an area for your mother to work. Since you've come to take a look, I assume you've talked to Lucy?"

"I phoned her."

Please, God, let Lucy be able to finish this project. This was supposed to be a special Christmas. My last one as a resident of Canyon Springs. But everything is snowballing out of control. Please?

She took a steadying breath. "And?"

"And…" Cody's brows formed a sympathetic,

inverted *V*. "She can't follow through on it. Dad's too sick. She needs to be there for him."

"But she signed a contract. Accepted payment."

"Yes, she's well aware of all that."

"Well, then, what—?"

"What am I doing here? I wanted to see how much she's done." Cody glanced toward the work area, then once again leveled a steady gaze on Paris. "And see how much *I* have left to do."

Chapter Four

A soft, startled breath escaped Paris's lips. Cody wasn't sure if that was good or bad. All he knew was that it pierced his heart and made him more determined to make good on his mother's commitment to the holiday gala. For Ma. For Paris.

She shot him a confused look. "You're taking over for your mother?"

"She feels badly about letting you down. Being unable to fulfill a promise isn't something she takes lightly."

He still marveled that Ma said Dad had agreed to help out, to do the construction for her. That sure wasn't the Leroy Hawk he knew.

"She asked you to do this?"

"I offered to do it when I realized how upset she was."

When I sensed how upset you would be.

"But your mother is an artist."

Cody chuckled. "That she is. And I'm not a half-bad one myself, if you'll recall."

He'd once garnered the courage to waylay Paris as she walked home alone from school one afternoon. He'd shown her a sketch he'd done while observing her from a far corner of study hall. The drawing was one of many where he'd done his best to capture her expressive eyes and her shimmering dark hair draping over her shoulders.

That day she'd stared for a long moment at the sketch he'd handed her, telling her she could keep it. She'd blushed furiously, thanked him, then hurried home without a backward glance.

Had she kept it? Or tossed it in the trash?

"You are," she said softly, her cheeks even now tinged a delicate pink, "a very good artist."

So she did remember.

"Ma has the staging designs worked out. All I have to do is build them. Everything will be true to the original plan the committee approved months ago."

She glanced uncertainly toward the work area, then at him. "Don't you have a job you have to get back to?"

He could tell it embarrassed her to ask. The older Hawk boys hadn't been known to stay with anything long. Where were they now? In Texas again? New Mexico? Barry had been in and out of who knows how many marriages and had done time in jail for violation of a restraining order. Carson had been in and out of trouble with the law as well and fathered more than a few illegitimate children.

"I do have a job, but it's flexible enough at the moment to let me remain in town a few weeks to help my mother. And *you*."

From the look in her eyes, he shouldn't have added that personal postscript. But it didn't much matter whether she liked it or not. He wasn't going to let Ma down and allow her reputation to be dragged down to the level of his dad and half brothers.

"Ma's subcontracting the project to me. If you'll make sure Harry the Gatekeeper knows I have approval so I can come and go here and at the clubhouse as time allows, I guarantee the staging will more than meet your expectations and your deadline."

He'd do it if he had to work twenty-four hours a day.

Could she tell that he had no expectations tacked onto his offer of assistance? Neither of them had alluded to that long-ago night when he'd poured out his heart to her, but it hung like an invisible barrier between them. As much as he'd like to spend every moment of his time in Canyon Springs with Paris, even with Dalton out of the picture he wouldn't attempt to insert himself into her world again as he'd done twelve years ago.

Doubt colored her eyes. "I'm not sure—"

"I'd say you could think it over and get back to

me later." He nodded toward the work area as his eyes remained locked on hers. "But there's no time to accommodate much thinking, let alone much 'later.' I need to get crackin'. And you need to get on out of here and let me get to work."

Cody's authoritative words still echoed through Paris's mind on Monday morning as she poured herself another glass of orange juice. They'd been spoken as if he were the boss and she an unwelcome intrusion on his valuable time.

You need to get on out of here and let me get to work.

She should have protested, should have told him the contract was with his mother, not him, and that the committee would make alternate arrangements. But what choice did she truly have with the gala now fewer than three weeks away? Bristling under the surface, she'd nevertheless obediently departed, stopping off at the gatehouse to inform Harry of Cody's project work and to authorize the use of Lucy's keycard.

She *should* be relieved. A decorating disaster had been averted at the midnight hour. Everything would be finished on time if Cody was true to his word, and there would be little need to interact with him. He'd made it clear he could handle it on his own and would brook no interference that might delay him in meeting his mother's obligations.

So why was she feeling anything but relief?

"Something on your mind, sweetheart?" Her father rose from the breakfast table to gaze out at the thickly pined acreage from the French doors of his sprawling log home. It had been her home again, too, ever since she'd cut short her junior year at Northern Arizona University and returned when Dad had what he referred to as "my ticker episode." After Mom's death, he hadn't taken good care of himself and had worked too hard. Following a heart bypass and a change in lifestyle facilitated by the diligence of his daughter, Paris hadn't returned to school—a decision she was increasingly coming to regret.

Dad turned away from a light flurry of snow that lent the view a Christmas-card beauty. "You seem distracted this morning."

"I'm mentally planning out my day," she said lightly, instinctively knowing her father wouldn't approve of Cody offering his services on behalf of the charity event. He'd hear of it soon enough, though, because she'd have to tell the committee tonight. Some—like Elizabeth—would doubt the wisdom of permitting him to take part. Trusting the job to the talented Lucy Hawk was one thing. A Hawk male was quite another.

She'd have to be prepared for pushback.

"Don't feel obligated to help with those weddings," her father stated, assuming that was the issue troubling her. "It's okay to change your mind.

There's not a soul in town who would fault you for not lending a hand."

"No, but…" Paris smoothed the cloth napkin in her lap. What Dad said was true. Anyone who'd read the local paper's gushing front-page article in which her engagement had been announced—and later experienced the shock of Dalton's death reverberating through the community—could guess at the pall which descended on her at the prospect of weddings.

"I think, though," she continued as her father leaned in to kiss her on the top of her head as he'd done since she was a little girl, "it's time I got over my aversion to weddings."

That's the conclusion she'd prayerfully come to Friday night and now, with Cody seeing to the decorating, she could once again conclude it was the right decision. Things had gone well enough with Macy on Saturday, hadn't they? Except for those awkward moments when the soon-to-be bride apologized for her perceived insensitivity. Unfortunately, Paris's strategy of wedding avoidance had only served to draw sympathy she didn't deserve.

Dad studied her a long moment. Widowed fourteen years ago when her mother's multiple sclerosis had finally taken its toll, he was a still-handsome man in his early sixties, his dark hair silvering at the temples. He'd caught the eye of more than a few women since Mom's passing. But not only had he not remarried, he never dated, unless you counted occasionally asking a friend or business associate to accompany him to an event. Most often he went alone. Not that anyone could ever replace Marna Perslow, but Paris had always thought Elizabeth would be a perfect match. Why, after her husband's death, had Dad never acted on what she sensed might be a mutual attraction?

Dad had to be lonely at times and that's likely why he threw himself too fully into his work, a fact that worried her at the thought of leaving him on his own when she left Canyon Springs. This morning a crease had formed across his forehead when she'd mentioned Cody Hawk's scheduled appointment and it hadn't yet smoothed.

"Don't let our good pastor pressure you," he said. "Sharon is entirely capable of handling things on her own and the other two young ladies can call on family and friends if needed. Everyone in town understands the pain weddings bring to you."

Actually, there *wasn't* a soul in town who understood her pain. Not the true source of it, anyway. Would involvement with the weddings, as her pastor had suggested, help her heal?

Nevertheless, she nodded as her father headed to his study, then she checked the time. With the office assistant out again today, she needed to get there by eight to cover the phones and front desk. But she'd promised to give Dad a hand with paperwork for sales he'd be closing on this week, so she could conveniently be in the back room when Cody arrived at nine-thirty.

Why couldn't she stop thinking about him?

She'd been surprised to glimpse him in church with his mother yesterday. But to her irritation, throughout the service—and afterward—she couldn't keep her thoughts from wandering to that long-ago night when he'd told her he loved her. Had always loved her. Would love her forever.

She gave a soft, scoffing laugh as she headed up the stairs to her room. *Teenagers.*

But her heart beat more quickly as she recalled in excruciating detail how he'd stared down at her that night. How she'd leaned in ever-so-slightly toward him, certain he'd kiss her. Even though she'd dutifully turned him down, she'd been mesmerized by the powerful yearning in his black-brown eyes.

But he hadn't kissed her.

Instead, he'd quirked a smile and stepped back as if pleased with what he'd read in her eyes. He'd brazenly delivered his line about her one day begging him to marry her. And then he was gone, leaving her stunned.

Cody had been clear on his long-term intentions that night. But what was he thinking now? And why did the prospect of his continued interest—or lack of it—unsettle her so?

"Thank you for your generosity, Mr. Perslow. But the Hawk family no longer takes charity. I'm more than willing to pay Dad's share of the insurance premium."

Cody sat across the desk from the owner of Perslow Real Estate, trying to figure out where the generous response of his father's employer was coming from. He'd expected resistance, maybe even an argument, but neither had been forthcoming. Even though Paris's father wasn't obligated by law due to the fact that he had fewer than fifty employees, he seemed more than willing to make concessions to accommodate Leroy Hawk.

"That's a commendable sentiment, Cody, but it's a nonissue. This isn't charity. I'd extend this offer to any employee who'd worked for me as long as your father has."

Sixteen years. That's longer than Dad had worked anyplace in his whole life. Even in Canyon Springs, he'd drifted from job to job for several years until Merle Perslow hired him on full-time when Cody was in eighth grade. Dad could be a diligent, skilled worker whose productivity outshone just about anybody—when he wasn't on a drinking binge. Cody grudgingly handed it to Mr. Perslow for his willingness not to see Dad's stroke as an opportunity to immediately kick him off the payroll.

Cody leaned forward. "I appreciate that, but you are aware, aren't you, that my father's situation may not be..." He hadn't seen Dad yet—concerned that his sudden appearance might trigger another stroke—but he didn't like to think of the robust Leroy as permanently disabled, his mental adeptness impaired and motor skills incapacitated. "His recovery is uncertain."

His likelihood of survival was still unclear.

Mr. Perslow gave a brisk nod. "Then we'll cross that bridge when we come to it, won't we?"

This was odd. Genuinely odd. But Cody had prayed for days that Paris's father would, if nothing else, be willing to let Cody continue paying his father's portion—or all—of the insurance premiums. He'd prayed, too, that his dad's position would be held open should he eventually be able to return, and that a paycheck would be forthcoming until it was determined if he had to go on permanent disability. Merle's response was more than Cody could have hoped for.

He stood and extended his hand to the older man who also rose to his feet. "Thank you...sir."

A faint smile touched Mr. Perslow's lips as they gripped hands, no doubt remembering the last time Cody had been in this office and flung that term of respect less than respectfully.

"Will you be in town long?"

Why did that question sound more loaded than a casual inquiry? "For a few weeks at least."

"I see." The older man cut him a sharp look as he ran his hand through his hair. The flecks of silver weren't the only thing indicating that twelve years had passed since their last meeting. He appeared older in other ways now. He was still trim and tanned, but there was a general air of world-weariness that had been present throughout their brief conversation.

Then, unexpectedly, a flash of the old Mr. Perslow lit his features as he pinned Cody with an uncompromising look. "My daughter's heart is fragile. There's someone else coming into her life now. Don't mess it up."

Cody's eyes narrowed as the icy words hung between them. A warning. It was almost as if he knew Cody had lain awake the past two nights since learning Paris hadn't married Dalton after all.

Even his days had been consumed with getting his head around this unexpected revelation. Sharon hadn't mentioned Paris's involvement with anyone, so Mr. Perslow could be lying about that. Then again, he wouldn't be surprised if she was seeing someone three and a half years after the death of her fiancé. Men must have lined up around the block, waiting for a suitable period of mourning to pass so they could make their move.

Hadn't he been contemplating that himself?

But now, as his resentful gaze met her father's, it became suddenly clear why he'd been so accommodating of Cody's requests on behalf of Leroy Hawk. His concessions had been a bribe to stay away from his daughter.

Before Cody could garner a response, the phone on the desk rang. Mr. Perslow frowned as he glanced down at the illuminated display, obviously irritated at the interruption. Then with a final cutting look at Cody he lifted the receiver, his tone at once warm and welcoming.

"Donald! Let me guess. Your wife has visions of a Canyon Springs Christmas dancing in her head and the two of you want to take another look at that condo."

Cody quietly walked out into the hallway and closed the office door behind him. He should have known Paris's father hadn't gone soft, that his generosity held an edge. A cunning purpose.

A muscle in his jaw tightened as anger flared and a too-familiar sense of shame pressed in. It was the same feeling he'd had when Paris's old man had caught him, at age sixteen, gazing longingly at the beauty of his fourteen-year-old daughter. In no uncertain terms, he'd let Cody know that a Hawk had no business "looking on the high shelf."

Cody had continued to look, if covertly. But even that last night when he'd longed to cup her beautiful face in his hands, to kiss her trembling lips, he'd held himself back.

Remembered he had no right.

Now to have her father suggest he'd barge into Paris's life and mess things up galled, and the fresh reminder that he was barred from pursuing her burned deep into his gut.

"Cody?"

The soft, questioning word echoed down the hall, jerking him from his thoughts. He turned away from the door, his spirits lifting at the vision before him. Hands on her slim hips, Paris's wide gray eyes studied him with open curiosity and, even in blue jeans and a bulky fisherman's sweater, she exuded a striking refinement, a delicate femininity. High-shelf material, indeed.

"Good morning, Paris." She hadn't been at the front desk when he'd arrived.

"Did everything go okay?"

"Your father's been...very helpful." He moved down the hallway to where she stood just inside the waiting room.

A dark brow rose. "I know you had concerns about your dad's situation."

"All addressed." With an unacceptable rider tacked on.

"I'm glad." She looked behind her where a middle-aged couple sat in the waiting area, admiring the Christmas tree. Then she again looked up at Cody. "Do you mind if we step outside for a few minutes?"

Although he hadn't knowingly made any promises to Mr. Perslow, they had shaken hands and it wouldn't bode well if her father saw him with Paris so soon after their conversation. Cody couldn't risk the insurance for Leroy Hawk being cancelled. Not until he had time to assess other options.

Nevertheless...

"Lead the way."

Chapter Five

Paris reached to the coatrack for her gray wool jacket.

"May I help with that?"

She glanced up uncertainly, but Cody's kind-hearted expression reassured. She nodded and he held out the coat behind her, taking care not to touch her as she slipped her arms into the sleeves.

"Thank you."

She started toward the door, then stopped, returning to the front desk to pick up a lidded, holiday-designed box, about twice the width of a shoe box. What had gotten her so flustered that she'd almost forgotten what she intended to give Cody?

They stepped outside where snowflakes danced merrily in the air, almost in time to the holiday carols coming from the overhead Main Street loudspeakers.

"What can I do for you, Paris?"

He looked especially handsome this morning,

but seemed somewhat on edge. Had things really gone as well with her father as he said they had?

She held out the box. "These are cookies for your mother to share with the hospital staff—and something extra for her, too."

He took the box from her, his expression uncertain. "Thank you."

"I remember her bringing homemade cookies those times my mother had to be hospitalized and how much the staff enjoyed them. I don't imagine your mother has any time to bake right now, so..."

He still didn't look as if he knew what to make of her gift. Almost suspicious, if she had to interpret his expression. But then life had probably taught Cody not to trust anyone.

"No, she doesn't have much time for herself these days." He placed his hand on top of the box. "She says the nurses have been great. Dad's not the easiest patient to care for, so she'll enjoy having something to give them as a thank-you."

Good. He finally got it.

"I imagine your dad was surprised to see you, wasn't he?"

"He..." Cody hesitated, as if unsure how his response would be taken. "He doesn't know I'm here yet."

Surprised, her brows arched. "You haven't gone to see him?"

He gripped the box more tightly. "I drove Ma to the hospital in Show Low a few days last week and on Sunday. But we're trying not to hit him with anything that might bring on another stroke."

"Like you suddenly showing up after twelve years," she said softly, the tension flickering through his eyes making her wish she hadn't brought up the subject in the first place.

"Right." He stared down at the cookie box and she could sense his emotions swirling through him. Dread at the thought of again facing his abusive father and shame that she might not think him a good son for putting off that inevitable encounter.

"I personally think that's a wise decision on your and your mother's part." She placed her hand on his forearm and his head jerked up, his eyes searching for truthfulness in her words. "You have to put his well-being first. There will be plenty of time for the two of you to get reacquainted."

Cody's grip on the box relaxed a fraction.

"Ma's mentioned to him a few times that I might come to visit. He doesn't react one way or another, so we're thinking I should stop in soon and see how it goes."

"Hopefully well. I'll be praying so."

"Thanks."

He glanced around, as if realizing they were talking in a public setting, as though suspecting someone might be observing their chat. What would be wrong with that? But she withdrew her hand from his arm and he took a step back.

He cleared his throat as his gaze again caught

hers. Softened. "I've been remiss in not expressing my sympathy for your loss, Paris."

Oh, no, not now. She didn't want this conversation to be about her, about concern for her grief.

"I knew you'd gotten engaged four years ago and assumed you and Dalton married. Until Sharon Dixon told me on Saturday about the car accident."

His mother hadn't told him years ago? He hadn't known when he'd come to her father's office on Friday? Why ever not? Everyone in town knew about it.

"Dalton was a good guy," he added.

"Yes, he was." At least Cody wasn't a gusher like many who assured her they understood her loss, who wanted to reminisce about her fiancé as a young boy, a teen, a man.

Cody lifted the lid on the cookie box, the mouth-watering scent of homemade molasses cookies sure to tempt even the strictest of dieting medical staff. A small envelope lay on top, inscribed to Lucy.

His smile quirked. "So you think you can trust me to get these to the hospital uneaten?"

Relieved at the change in subject, she playfully placed her hands on her hips. "You'd better, mister."

The corners of his eyes crinkled. "Or what?"

"Or...I'll tell your mother, and then you'll be in big trouble."

"That's a threat intended to make me shake in my boots?" He grinned, then bumped the envelope with his finger. "What's in there?"

"Gift cards to Wyatt's Grocery and the gas station. I'm sure with the expenses your father is incurring and the many trips to—"

"Thank you, but Hawks don't take charity." Cody's smile dissolved as he snapped the box lid closed and thrust it toward her.

Charity? What was he talking about? She gently pushed the box back, her eyes firmly meeting his. "This isn't charity. It's a gift for your mother to use where she needs it most."

He opened the box again and extracted the envelope. "I'll take the cookies to her, but not the gift cards."

Confused at his reaction, she put her hands behind her back, refusing the envelope he held out. "I don't want them back. You're being silly."

"You think so?"

"Your mother does nice things for people in this town and this is a small way of showing appreciation in a practical way."

"I value your concern but, like I said, Hawks don't take handouts anymore." His jaw hardened. "If there's anything she needs, I'll see that she gets it."

She folded her arms. Why was he being so stubborn? "This isn't a handout."

"Let's not quibble over semantics, Paris," he said quietly as he tucked the envelope in the snug space between her folded arms, then gave the box lid a firm pat. "I'll see that Ma gets these. Maybe minus a cookie or two."

He winked. But his attempt to inject humor fell flat with her.

"Please don't be this way, Cody. You know I—"

"Your thoughtfulness is appreciated. Let it go at that." He lifted his hand for a lighthearted salute, then turned away, the cookie box tucked under his arm as he headed down the street.

Stubborn, pride-filled man. Why was he acting as if she'd likened his mother to a panhandler on the street?

"Cody!" It was all she could do not to stamp her foot like a two-year-old in a tantrum.

He lifted his hand again in a parting wave, but didn't stop or look back. Kept right on walking.

She drew an irritated breath. She hadn't even had a chance to ask him how things were going with the Christmas project, if he still thought it doable or if she needed to recruit additional volunteers.

But she wasn't about to chase after him.

Conscious of Paris's exasperated gaze and guilt-ridden for not having yet visited his father, Cody climbed into his truck. He brushed the snow from his hair, hoping the high country didn't get heavy snow while he was here. He had his eye on a new Ford F-150 but, with his vehicle in the shop, he'd been forced to commandeer one of his business partner's old junkers. It couldn't be counted on in significant snowfall.

He checked for traffic and backed out, but didn't allow himself to glance in Paris's direction. Then he pressed his foot to the accelerator and headed for his folks' place.

He didn't think of it as home.

Dad and Ma still lived in a double-wide trailer that they'd settled in when Cody had been in ninth grade and his half brothers—who only lived with their father when their mother periodically kicked them out of her place in New Mexico—were long gone.

Looking back, where had his folks gotten the money for a down payment? He wouldn't ask. Better not to know. Leroy Hawk had done time in Texas for forging his employer's signature when Cody was a second grader. Another time for attempted extortion.

How had Ma endured it?

He knew it was foolish, but he couldn't help but feel responsible. When he was a kid he'd overheard her telling someone he was a preemie, but it didn't take a mathematician to figure out his folks had to get married. Maybe if he hadn't come along, Ma would have married someone more deserving of her.

Cody shook his head as he rounded a treed curve, the windshield wipers beating a sporadic rhythm against the lightly falling snow. By the time he'd entered school here midautumn of fifth grade, he'd been pulled in and out of schools in three different states and five different towns. It was amazing he'd managed to graduate at all. He owed that to his mother—and to his own stubborn streak.

And speaking of stubbornness... He glanced at the box on the seat beside him. Had he been wrong to turn down the gift cards for his mother? Paris meant well and he hadn't intended to hurt her feelings as he suspected he had. God only knew how many people had slipped a little something extra to Ma in the years he'd been gone. After his departure from town, he hadn't had much to spare for her at first. He should be thankful, not resentful, that people cared.

Paris couldn't have known her thoughtfulness would push a hot button. Touch his pride. He'd overreacted.

Lord, I've got to stop taking things like this so personally, seeing it as a slap in the face every time someone is moved to an act of kindness on my or my family's behalf.

As he pulled onto the property that his mother had optimistically named Hawk's Hope in deference to a Canyon Springs property-naming tradition, his cell phone chimed.

"Yo, Trev. Any word yet?"

"Not yet," Cody's business partner, Trevor Cane, confirmed, "I hoped maybe you'd been contacted directly."

He could picture his stocky, well-groomed friend pacing the tiles of his Phoenix patio. It would be a balmy sixty-five degrees down there today, quite a contrast to the mountain country a few hours north and six thousand feet higher.

Cody chuckled. "If I get the call, you'll know when I know. That wouldn't be anything I'd keep to myself."

"I guess I'm getting antsy. Do you think we'll hear anything soon or is that wishful thinking?"

Cody was antsy, too, although he wouldn't admit it to Trevor. So much rode on this business deal, and hearing a "yes" would sure be the answer to a truckload of prayers.

"It might not be until after the first of the year. I advise you to sit back, relax and enjoy your family while you can. If this goes through as we hope, there's going to be more than enough work to keep us both occupied for some time to come."

"How much longer will you be up there?"

"At least until Christmas. Things are still touch-and-go with Dad."

He glanced toward the trailer. He'd started cleaning up the property, clearing out old tires, broken equipment and other assorted junk. But there were repairs still to be made to the trailer itself, fencing and outbuildings. Maybe one day, though, he'd get Ma that cabin in the pines Dad always promised her.

Cody reached for the cookie box, then stepped

out into the lightly falling snow. "Ma's running interference between Dad and the hospital staff, trying to keep him calm and them from calling the cops."

Nicotine and alcohol withdrawal and a stroke on top of that. Not a nice combo.

"But the good thing is—" Cody gave a bitter chuckle as he unlocked the front door and stepped inside, his nostrils flaring with distaste at the lingering scent of stale cigarettes "—his right arm is incapacitated, so he won't be swinging it at me anytime soon."

"Man, it had to be tough growing up that way."

For almost a dozen years, he and Trev had been as close as God probably intended real brothers to be. He hadn't had any contact with his half brothers since he'd been in middle school and they'd gone out on their own. But his friendship with Trevor had more than made up for that lack.

"Yeah, well, I guess this is where I'm supposed to say growing up like that made me who I am today. Right?" Cody placed the cookie box on the dining table.

Trevor huffed a laugh. "That's one way of looking at it."

It was the only way to look at it, otherwise it made no sense. No sense at all. Just like coming back to town and discovering Paris hadn't married...

As if picking up on his line of thought, Trevor

ventured deeper. "So, did that dream gal of yours and her hubby come home for Thanksgiving?"

Even though he'd long ago faced reality and dated a number of women since leaving Canyon Springs, when Paris had gotten engaged his friend and his friend's new wife had been there to pick up the pieces. They'd reeled Cody back in when he'd foolishly acted out in ways for which he was now ashamed. Trevor and Maribeth had played an instrumental role in directing his steps toward God, for which he'd be forever grateful.

"Actually...she's living here. But not married." He navigated his way across the room to slide open the door to the rear of the property and let the cold December air hit him full in the face.

"You're kidding. She's divorced already?"

"Nope. Never married." He stepped onto the snow-wet deck. "The guy was killed in a car accident before the wedding."

Trevor gave a low whistle. "Have you talked to her?"

"I have."

"And?"

He ran his hand along the deck railing, brushing off the thin layer of snow with his bare hand and noting a need for a good sanding and paint job. "Apparently she's involved with someone else now."

"Sorry, bud. The timing stinks. But I hope by seeing her again you got closure. You know, that you now recognize she's no longer the girl of your adolescent infatuation."

Cody drew a long breath. Trev was right. Paris was no longer the girl of his teenage fantasies.

She was the woman of his grown-man dreams.

Chapter Six

"Remember to stop and smell the roses, Paris," Dad playfully admonished on Thursday morning when he'd caught her staring at her lengthy "to do" list. "Or the pine trees, rather. Remember, this *is* the Christmas season. Ho ho ho."

She smiled indulgently. That was easily said by someone who didn't lift a finger to help with holiday preparations. When Mom had been alive he'd left that up to her. Now it fell to his daughter.

"By the way, honey, great breakfast as always. Thanks." He gave her a thumbs-up, then headed off to work for an early morning meeting.

Guilt gnawed at his words of appreciation. He'd be fending for himself soon enough…would he make the effort to eat healthy or resort to processed foods and dining out?

With a sigh, she again picked up her list from the kitchen counter. She had more than enough to keep herself occupied all day what with Dad's open house taking place tomorrow afternoon and evening. While he was okay with some items being catered, he preferred the homemade touch and enjoyed bragging about it.

Paris had completed the grocery shopping after work yesterday and decorated the house over a series of evenings this week. Yes, there were still more than enough activities to fill her day even though she'd deliberately not scheduled any property showings. And yet…

Before she knew it, she was driving through the gates of Pine Shadow Ridge in the predawn light. Despite Cody's reassurance, as the event's head she should monitor his progress and report back to her fellow committee members. As suspected, there had been more than a few unhappy campers at Monday night's meeting when she'd enlightened them on Cody's role.

If Dad had heard about it, though, he'd kept silent, which made her think he was still in the dark. That wouldn't last long, though, so she needed evidence to back up the wisdom of accepting Cody's assistance.

Inside the maintenance building, she stopped to speak to a few men who were adjusting a snow blade on a pickup truck. Then she made her way to the far corner where each year a makeshift workshop was set up for the Christmas event. Stacks of lumber, sawhorses, paint cans and brushes were now organized in an orderly fashion. Cody's touch, no doubt, as they hadn't appeared as well-arranged on Saturday. He'd already framed a number of the log cabin facades Lucy had illustrated in her design.

A High Country Christmas.

That theme had been Paris's idea. It seemed appropriate for what would likely be her last in the mountain town she'd grown up in. She ran her hand up the side of one of the sturdy frames as a knot tightened in her stomach. She didn't know what she planned to do when she left here. Return to school? Get a job—doing what? Continuing to sell real estate? She only knew that, as hard as it would be to leave, it was time to say goodbye to Canyon Springs.

"Well, Paris—" A low masculine voice close behind startled her from her reverie. "Do things meet with your approval?"

By the fact that she was here at this hour, it was evident she didn't trust him.

It was clear, too, from the guilty look in her eyes, that she'd come early thinking he wouldn't be here so she could snoop around. But he'd been up at his usual hour, touching base with Trevor who was also an early riser. Now he had a window of time to make progress on the project.

Despite their differences of opinion on Monday, however, you wouldn't catch him complaining about Paris keeping him from his work as he'd done the last time she'd been here. Dressed in a plaid skirt and tall suede boots, the rest of her was bundled in a fawn-colored, faux-fur jacket that made her look as huggable as a teddy bear.

She smelled good, too.

"Good morning, Cody. You're coming right along here, I see."

He smiled to himself, noting she'd ignored his somewhat accusatory question. Nor did she broach the subject of the rejected gift cards, where their last conversation had ended. "This part is going fairly quickly. It's the painting and detail work that will be most time consuming."

That would also be the part the committee would eye most critically.

"I was wondering if you'd like a quick tour of the clubhouse where the gala will be held. I didn't show you around on Saturday."

"Thanks, but I gave myself an unguided tour after you left. I needed to take measurements and get a feel for the space to make sure Ma's designs-come-to-life are proportionally appropriate."

"Then you're a step ahead of me." She turned again to the framing he'd completed. "So you'll fill in the openings with fabric or canvas you can paint?"

"Actually, I think I can do better than that." He stepped to a worktable where his mother's sketches fanned over the surface. "I've checked out options to attach lightweight tubing to the framework.

Then a troweled-on substance that sticks securely to the surface will add a loglike texture. It should then be easy to spray paint a base color with only highlights and lowlights added by hand for further dimension."

Paris's eyes brightened, envisioning what he was talking about, and his heart lifted in gratification that she got it. He wouldn't have to defend his strategy or try to talk her into it.

"I like that idea, Cody."

Paris smiled up at him and his heart further lightened. That smile had been his sought-after reward for more years than he could count. You'd have thought its power to sway him would have diminished. But maybe his reaction to it was merely a residual teenage crush, a lingering flicker of hope that had dogged him for too many years?

Who was the man she was seeing now anyway? No doubt he'd be a prominent member of this community or a neighboring one. Did he know him? Who could he ask without appearing too interested?

"It's not that your mother's original plan isn't a good one," she added, "but the three-dimensional aspect will add so much."

He basked in her approval. "That's the plan."

A smile touched her lips and he got the impression she was relieved. She might not yet trust him—after all, she didn't know him now any more than he knew her—but he was determined to prove she could count on him. To prove a Hawk was as good as his word.

"I know your mother appreciates having you here. You know, to help with the Christmas gala and with your Dad's situation, too."

"I'm doing my best."

Did Paris recall the bad blood between father and son? The bruises he'd once revealed to her? He sure remembered how as a grade-schooler she'd cautiously reached out gentle fingers to caress the swollen, purpled skin along his rib cage. How tears had pooled in her eyes. He hadn't wanted her to feel sorry for him, though, and never showed her again. Never spoke of it.

Cody pulled his thoughts back to the present and, as if determined to lighten the mood, Paris cut him an almost playful look that caught him off guard. "I suppose—"

"Paris! I thought that looked like your SUV. What brings you out here so early this morning?"

They turned to see a man not many years older than Cody striding toward them, the superior quality of his wool jacket and the dismissive look he gave Cody spelling out his economic equality with Paris.

Cody's eyes narrowed. Was this the man she was seeing?

"Hello, Owen." Paris's smile widened as if genuinely happy at his arrival, but when the man reached her side, she didn't fling her arms around him or plant a kiss on his lips when he leaned in to hug her. But that didn't mean this Owen guy wasn't the one Mr. Perslow had mentioned as "coming into her life."

"Now, don't you look adorable in that furry jacket, my dear." Owen's eyes warmed as he gazed down at her. "Like a cuddly teddy bear."

Paris laughed, but Cody gritted his teeth at the assessment mirroring his own. No doubt this Owen character noticed her shapely booted legs as well, but knew better than to comment on them. At least in front of Cody.

"Owen, I want you to meet Cody Hawk," Paris said, laying a hand on the newcomer's arm. "Cody, this is Owen Fremont, one of the newest investors in Pine Shadow Ridge."

"Hawk, did you say?" An arrogant brow rose as the two men shook hands, both of them obviously sizing each other up and finding the other lacking.

"Yes," Paris continued, unaware of or choosing to ignore Owen's haughty tone. But at least she hadn't introduced the guy as her boyfriend or fi-ancé, so there was a good chance their relationship hadn't been signed, sealed and delivered. "Cody's mother is the decorative designer of this year's Christmas gala and he's helping us out while he's in town."

"I see."

Probably more than Cody wanted him to see. It

wouldn't take a genius to recognize that another man had taken notice of this very attractive woman.

Paris motioned to the wooden structures next to her. "Cody's framing up the faux log cabins for our high country Christmas theme. He's brimming with ideas."

"I'm sure he is," Owen said dryly, casting a subtle warning glance in Cody's direction before turning again to Paris. "So you're not working this morning? We could do breakfast at the clubhouse, if you like."

Obviously Cody wasn't included in the invitation.

"I'm sorry, but I've had breakfast and I do have to go to the office for a while. Then I have a mile-long list of things I have to see to." She noted the time on her watch, then snuggled her jacket collar more closely around her neck. "I came out early hoping to catch Cody so he could update me on his progress."

Would that be a regular visit he could count on?

"Some other time, then." Owen offered his arm. "May I see you to your car?"

Paris hesitated, glancing uncertainly at Cody, then nodded and slipped her arm into Owen's. "You're doing a great job, Cody. Your mother— and the committee—will be pleased."

"Thank you."

But Owen didn't look pleased in the least, and a surge of satisfaction welled up in Cody. No, he wouldn't attempt to mess things up for Paris, but maybe the self-satisfied Owen would manage that on his own.

"Let's be on our way, then." Owen tugged at her arm. "I know you don't want to be late for work."

"Thanks again, Cody," Paris called back as the pair made their way across the open space toward the door.

Cody watched grimly as they exited the building. Owen Fremont. A city slicker with cash to burn and a greedy eye on Paris. At least the guy she was involved with wasn't someone Cody knew. That would have been even harder to stomach.

"Better put those eyes back in your head, Hawk." An amused voice echoed through the high-ceilinged space.

Cody swung around to see it was Jim Harper who'd called out to him from where he was tinkering with the snow blade on a pickup truck. Jim had been in school with him, an okay guy but not one Cody had been friends with—probably because he'd caught him ogling Paris on occasion. But they'd visited this week and seemed to get along fine now.

Cody cupped his ear. "What's that?"

Jim laughed. "You heard me, buddy. You don't stand a chance and you know it."

Shaking his head, Cody waved Jim off good-naturedly, then turned to start on the next few hours of work. He'd like to get the framing of the cabins done by tomorrow, then move on to securing the mock logs. He couldn't stay here all day, though, as he'd told Mom he'd stop in to see Dad.

Man, he didn't look forward to that first encounter.

He placed a board across the sawhorses, recalling the pretty picture Paris had made in her furry jacket, her dark hair loosely tumbling over the collar, her eyes bright and soft lips smiling her pleasure at his progress.

He took a labored breath and reached for another board.

Jim was right.

He could dream those teenage dreams all he wanted, but they wouldn't go any further. Even if that Owen dude hadn't been staking his claim, Cody didn't stand a chance. What could the prettiest woman in town, who'd once handed him a box at a community food bank, possibly see in him?

Lord, why'd You have to call me back to Canyon Springs right now? Why'd Dad have to go and have a stroke so Ma can't follow through on her commitment?

Cody let out a pent-up breath. He needed to buck up and face reality. God likely had a sweet gal tucked somewhere out of sight who'd been impatiently waiting for him to get his act together. He'd been slow coming to God and slow to allow God to heal the animosity he'd long felt toward his father and was only now coming to terms with.

Maybe facing his teenage feelings was a test, something that had to be done to set him free to love and be loved by the little lady God had in mind for him all along. He wouldn't want to miss out because he couldn't grow up and let go of an adolescent infatuation.

Was reality finally sinking in or was he subconsciously backing off because he feared Paris's father would rescind offers made on Dad's behalf? Cody wasn't yet in a position to take on the medical bills, long-term care or any debt his folks may have incurred through the years.

Either way, Paris clearly wasn't in his future.

He reached for a hammer and nail.

He could do this. Guard his heart. With God's help, anyway. It would be easier, though, if Paris didn't come around again.

But he couldn't bring himself to pray that she wouldn't.

Chapter Seven

"Oh, the weather outside is frightful..." Paris hummed the final bars of a favorite Christmas tune as the windshield wipers slashed away soggy snowflakes.

Although menacing clouds had descended, the highway wasn't too bad. With all she had to do for tomorrow, she hadn't planned to make an afternoon trek to Show Low. But she'd gotten a call from Reyna and promised she'd stop by the hospital before the weekend, drop off a few things she needed and discuss details of the upcoming weddings.

She was thrilled the Christmas gala preparations were coming along because of Cody, as suddenly all three brides needed her attention. The dress Sharon ordered online three months ago was abruptly unavailable. With so many motels and rental properties closed for the winter, Abby was having difficulty finding enough rooms for Brett's huge family. And Macy's mother suddenly refused to make the trip to Arizona, which wore on the bride's increasingly frazzled nerves.

"Why," Paris said aloud as she slowed to enter town, "do people put themselves through this? Why not elope and save themselves the grief?"

In her case, however—had things not ended in tragedy—*not* eloping would have been a blessing. Seven months of attending to ceremony, reception and honeymoon details finally gave God the time needed to catch her attention. All the preparations had to be undone, of course. Reservations canceled, deposits forfeited. Her gown and the dresses she'd purchased for her bridesmaids donated to charity.

But *had* it been God, or her own fears that brought her up short? Paris adjusted the wiper speed as she stared through the streaked windshield at the gloomy day. Should she have gone through with the wedding, keeping her mouth shut and not asking Dalton to return for a heart-to-heart talk? Had she been too self-centered, thinking only about what *she* needed out of the relationship rather than focusing on what she should be putting into it? *Could* she have made Dalton happy?

There were no answers—and never would be.

Once inside the medical center, Paris asked directions to Reyna's room. Fighting back the sounds and scents that reminded her too vividly of her mother's frequent hospital stays that last year of her life, she silently whispered a prayer of thanksgiving that Mom had passed away quietly in Canyon

Springs. Although he never said as much, Paris believed that's why Dad built a new home a few years later. While she found comfort in the memories shared during her mother's last days in hospice care, Dad likely wanted relief from them. To not walk into a room and remember...

As she stepped out of the elevator, a feminine voice with a soft Texan twang called to her.

"Miz Perslow? What brings you here? Your father is okay, I hope."

She turned to see Cody's mother, Lucy Hawk, who was maybe a decade younger than Dad. Not surprisingly, she looked tired today and it was tempting to cheer her with the gift cards Paris had tucked in her purse. But no, she wouldn't risk appearing disrespectful of Cody no matter how misguided his opinions might be.

"I'm here to see Reyna Kenton."

"Bless your heart." Lucy's gaze warmed as she brushed back her sandy-brown, chin-length bob. "She's in need of cheering up. She hopes to go home soon, but her doctor isn't making promises."

"She certainly doesn't want to be released prematurely and wind up back here again."

The older woman's gaze softened to a tenderness directed at Paris. "Which is why it's such a blessing you're stepping in to help with the weddings at Canyon Springs Christian. I know it's not easy for you. Many difficult memories."

Paris redirected the conversation before it veered

toward memories of Dalton. "Cody said there hadn't been much change in your husband's condition."

"No, unfortunately. I do thank you for being understanding about my inability to follow through on the Christmas gala."

"You couldn't know this would happen to your husband. But you'll be pleased to know Cody is making rapid headway."

Lucy smiled at the confirmation. "I don't know what I'd do without him right now, but he has important things needing attention elsewhere."

Like what? And why was she wondering if those important things had to do with a woman?

"I doubt," Paris pointed out, "that Cody would do anything he didn't want to do."

Lucy laughed. "True."

"Did I hear my name taken in vain?"

Cody stepped out of the elevator, an insulated cup of coffee in his hand, and Paris's heart gave an unexpected leap. He was dressed as he had been that morning, in jeans, work boots, a red flannel shirt and a black insulated vest. His attire set off his rugged good looks to perfection.

She'd enjoyed their brief visit earlier in the day, although it ended awkwardly with Owen Fremont insisting he walk her to her car. They didn't know each other that well, but Owen could be pushy at times.

With a grateful smile, Cody's mother accepted the lidded cup he handed to her. "Paris tells me you're making strides on the project I dumped in your lap."

He shrugged. "I volunteered, remember?"

"You did." Lucy's eyes flickered briefly to Paris, their expression hinting that something disquieting had crossed her mind. Then she again looked up at her son, injecting a teasing lilt into her words. "I intend to inspect everything to see how closely you've followed my design."

"Great. Two women looking over my shoulder." But from that lazy smile, he didn't appear too bothered by it.

Lucy glanced at the wall clock. "I'd better check on your father again. Thank you for the coffee. They keep this place like an icebox."

Her son's brows lowered. "How late do you plan to stay today? The sun sets shortly after five and you know how the roads can get after dark. I'll follow you home."

She leveled a troubled look at him. "I'll only be here long enough for you to see your father…and to deal with what may come of that."

The corners of Cody's mouth dipped. "I'll be in there in a few minutes."

Lucy's apprehensive gaze flickered again to Paris, then back to her son. "Take your time."

Something was bothering Ma and it wasn't only Dad. Looking down at Paris in her teddy-bear jacket and stylish boots, her French-braided hair and makeup enhancing the natural beauty she'd been born with, he had a feeling he knew what it was.

But Ma didn't need to worry. He had things under control and his heart under wraps.

"I take it you're here to see someone—and not my old man."

A smile touched Paris's lips. "Our pastor's wife, Reyna. She's being treated for pneumonia."

"I heard about that at church on Sunday. Sounded bad."

Paris glanced down the hallway as if casting for a topic to continue the conversation. Or maybe a way to end it? He should help her out since Owen wasn't around to lend a hand this time.

"I guess I'd better join my mother so I can get her back on the road before dark."

"I'll be praying, Cody." Paris looked up at him with surprising understanding. "I know this can't be easy."

Sort of like the past she was confronting by helping with the weddings? When he'd stopped by Dix's on his way here, Sharon commented that Paris hadn't involved herself with weddings since Dalton's death, but she thought overseeing three upcoming events was a good sign that Paris was healing.

"Walking into Dad's hospital room isn't something I look forward to, but it's one of the reasons I returned to town—to make my peace with Leroy

Hawk." From the second Ma called about Dad's stroke he knew, like it or not, God was giving him a warning. Dad could easily have died, an opportunity like today forever lost.

Paris impulsively caught his hand in both of hers. She gave it a quick squeeze, then released it. "Everything will be fine."

She smiled, her eyes beaming encouragement. Then she turned away and headed down the hall.

He moved in the opposite direction, the fingers of the hand she'd clasped now gripped tightly as he took his time walking to Dad's room. He'd never held her hand before, but he'd always wondered how it would feel in his.

Nice. Real nice.

At his father's open door he halted out of sight, inhaling the sharp, antiseptic odors around him. Dad had only gotten out of ICU this week, but was situated not far from the nurses' station. Would he turn his face away in silence at the arrival of his son or shake his fist in red-faced anger?

You called me here, Lord. Here I am.

He rapped his knuckles on the door frame as he stepped into the room. "Hey, Dad."

As his mother looked anxiously from father to son, Cody's gaze raked the sterile surroundings. Unlike rooms of other patients he'd passed on the way to this one, there were no balloon bouquets, no flowers. No get-well words of encouragement tacked above the bed. No family photos, posters or cards.

Just cold, bare walls.

A muscle tightened in Cody's throat as he drew his thoughts from the cheerless environment and forced himself to look his father in the eye. It was the first time since the night Dad, angered that Cody had turned down Mr. Perslow's job offer, had kicked him out of the house. Almost as big as his father by then, he'd caught Dad off-guard when he backed him against the garage wall and told him that with any luck they'd never see each other again—unless Ma wasn't treated right and he was forced to return and make good on his promise.

Please don't let my showing up cause another stroke.

The man now staring him down struggled unsuccessfully to sit up in bed. Leroy Hawk, while still broad-shouldered and brawny, was no longer the powerful, menacing man of Cody's memories. His face was severely drawn and pale, his eyes shadowed and sunken into their sockets. His right arm lay motionless, helpless, at his side.

Cody had known it was bad. His mother had warned that Dad retained impaired movement on his left side, but the right was entirely immobile. His speech patterns were hesitant, slurred, the words not always what he intended to say. Once-sharp mental faculties had dulled.

But Cody hadn't been prepared for the reality of it.

Ma placed a gentling hand on his father's arm, and Dad ceased his fruitless efforts to gain a seated position and settled back against the pillows. But his eyes never left Cody's, their expression everchanging from the moment he'd stepped through the door.

Surprise. Anger. Humiliation. Resignation.

"Come…" The intended smile was a grotesque grimace as Dad struggled for garbled words. "…kill…me?"

Most might not make out what he'd said. But Cody knew. A sense of shame for the teenage threat he'd made stabbed his heart. Then again, he shouldn't have been forced to issue the ultimatum. That was Dad's doing.

"Naw." Cody swallowed, then managed a half smile as he motioned to the bed with its tubes and monitoring paraphernalia. "Looks like you came close to doing a good job of that on your own."

"Did…didn't I?" The laugh emanating from the drawn-down, misshapen lips wasn't much more than a puff of air.

Cody took a few steps closer, but halted when his father's expression darkened.

With a tight smile, his mother patted Dad's arm again. "Cody's taken a few days off work to come check on us."

The wheezing sound might have been a disbelieving snort.

Ma's gaze flickered apologetically to Cody.

"I talked to Merle Perslow," Cody ventured, hoping the assurance that things on the work front were secure might give Dad peace of mind. "The paychecks will keep coming. Your insurance is covered. He's being pretty accommodating."

Dad's lips curled downward and a glint of self-satisfied humor lit his eyes. "Just…bet…is."

Cody glanced at his mother, hoping to receive a cue from her. Maybe a topic of conversation he could pursue or a hint that he should move on, that more shouldn't be expected of today's visit.

"Well, Leroy, it's time Cody and I head out. It's been snowing off and on this afternoon and Cody doesn't want me driving alone after dark. He'll follow me back home."

Dad grunted, then felt along the bed with his left hand until his fingers reached those of his wife. He squeezed them in a weak grip as he struggled to smile. She smiled back.

A knot jerked in Cody's stomach at that unexpected gesture of tenderness. He'd forgotten that when Dad hadn't been drinking, he'd treated Ma like a queen.

"You're ready then, Ma?"

She slipped her hand from her husband's and stood, then leaned over to kiss him on the forehead.

"You behave yourself tonight, Leroy. Don't give the night staff any trouble, you hear me?"

A sound that might have been a laugh escaped Dad's lips. "Back…tomorrow?"

"If the weather holds."

"I'll beg, borrow or steal a four-wheel drive," Cody assured, "if that's what it takes to get her here, Dad."

His father's now-drowsy gaze met Cody's, but he didn't reply. Then he closed his eyes and sank farther back into his pillows.

Cody's mother smiled sadly at her husband for a long moment, then picked up her coat and purse from a nearby chair and followed Cody into the hallway. He slipped his arm around her as they headed silently to the elevator.

Once inside the enclosed space, Cody pressed the down button. "He didn't seem overjoyed to see me, but at least he didn't keel over when I walked in."

"He was happy you'd come." His mother patted his arm. "I could tell."

Yeah, right. Ma was only trying to make him feel better, attempting to ease the shock of seeing Dad laid up like that, his face and limbs distorted, his mobility drastically impaired. It was worse than he'd imagined. An outdoorsman, Dad had always been robust, active. Fit. He'd been fast on his feet and threw a mean punch.

The elevator doors opened on ground level and

Cody motioned to his mother to exit first. "He has to hate being here. Being like that."

Ma nodded as Cody helped her into her coat. "Thank you for coming today. I thought things went well. God is good."

"I don't want to make a nuisance of myself, but I'd like to come back. You know, if you think that would be okay."

Today had been a start, but he and Dad had things to talk over. He wouldn't push it, though, and risk upsetting him.

"It would be more than okay, but don't feel you have to be here every day or provide transportation for me. I don't expect that. Seeing to the Christmas gala is what's allowing me to be here now. I can't thank you enough."

"I'll do anything I can to help. You know that."

Ma paused as they reached the exit to the parking lot. "Paris is a sweet girl. Beautiful inside and out."

"I agree on both counts."

Her eyes hesitantly met his. "You will be careful, won't you, Cody?"

Did she, like Merle Perslow, think he'd barge in and disrupt Paris's relationship with Owen? That he wouldn't be sensitive to what she'd been through with the death of her fiancé? "What do you mean?"

"We've never talked about it, but I know you've cared for her ever since you were a boy."

That obvious, was it? Cody forced a chuckle.

"There's probably not a kid in existence who hasn't lived through a crush."

"No. But I don't want to see my big boy get hurt."

So, like everyone else on the planet, she didn't think he stood a chance. That he'd only wind up harming himself if he didn't steer clear of the pretty Paris Perslow.

"You don't need to worry. I'm a grown man now."

"I know that. I just—"

He leaned over to give her a quick hug. "You still see me as a fifth grader being sent home the first day of school for misbehavior on the behalf of a cute third-grade girl."

She smiled up at him. "You walked through the door with a bloody nose and stars in your eyes."

He imagined it impossible for a male of any age not to get stars in his eyes when he looked at Paris.

He gave his mother another reassuring squeeze. "Stop your worrying, Ma."

There was nothing to worry about. Not a thing.

Chapter Eight

The soothing piano notes of "O Little Town of Bethlehem" drifted back to the kitchen where Paris had dropped in to check behind the scenes of the open house.

"I don't know who he is, Paris," Carrie, one of her teenage helpers stated, "but if you don't want him, I get dibs."

"What are you talking about?" Paris laughed as she removed another tray of hot water chestnuts wrapped in bacon from the oven, their sizzling aroma scenting the air. She couldn't seem to keep the warming dishes filled with them. Next year she'd know to double the popular recipe.

No. Not next year. She wouldn't be here to play hostess for the open house.

Pushing aside a ripple of unease, she set the tray on top of the stove and turned to where Carrie peeped out a front window of the log home's kitchen. Dressed in black slacks and a white shirt with a satin bow tie, her hair pulled back with an ebony ribbon, Carrie and the other two girls hired for the open house looked efficient and neatly attractive. All tattoos that might offend her father's more conservative guests were concealed by the crisp, long sleeves.

"Please tell me he's not married, Paris."

"Who?" Paris squeezed in beside Carrie to peer between the wooden slats. Ponderosa pines rose in silhouetted majesty in the fading daylight and solar fixtures along the walkway to the cabin's broad porch glowed softly. Leafless aspens sparkled with tiny fairy lights winding up their white trunks. A few more guests who'd left their cars along the curving drive approached, laughing and bundled against the cold, but she recognized all of them.

"You don't mean Sharlene Odel's cousin, do you?" She couldn't imagine anything about the middle-aged Andy that would elicit oohs and aahs from a seventeen-year-old girl.

"No." Carrie rolled her eyes, her tone offended.

"I don't see anybody else."

"Where'd he go?" The teen maneuvered for a better view. "Oh, there he is. To the far right now, coming up the drive along the trees. It looks like he's heading around to the side door."

A guest coming in the back way, to the entrance between the house and garage?

Paris angled for a better look, then her breath caught.

Cody. And he was carrying something.

Suddenly self-conscious as she listened for a knock at the side entrance, Paris moved back to the stove and picked up a spatula to sweep the water chestnuts into a bowl.

"Who is he?" Carrie pressed. "Do you know him?"

Paris handed her the serving bowl. "His name is Cody Hawk."

"Cody," the teen whispered, her eyes going dreamy. "Is he—?"

Paris laughed. "No, he's not married."

Or at least she assumed he wasn't. She couldn't help but notice he didn't wear a ring, but that didn't mean he wasn't spoken for.

"In that case, I'll be back in a minute—with my wedding gown." Carrie batted her eyes in an exaggerated manner. "I've got to meet this guy and set the date before Madison or Brianna spot him."

Carrie spun toward the door, then abruptly halted, her forehead wrinkling. "Did you say Cody *Hawk?* Like as in *Leroy* Hawk?"

"I did."

Everyone in town knew Leroy or had at least heard of him and his boys by reputation—even this girl a decade younger than Paris. Poor Cody.

"He's one of Leroy's sons."

Carrie groaned, her once-eager expression now crumpling. "You're kidding me, right?"

Paris shook her head.

"Just my luck." The girl grimaced. "There's something majorly wrong with a world that gives a man who looks like that to a father like Leroy Hawk."

Paris couldn't agree more.

Dejected, Carrie again turned away, then paused. "What's he doing here at your party?"

A firm knock sounded at the side door.

"He must be making a delivery."

Carrie sighed. "Great. The hired help. I sure know how to pick 'em."

As the girl departed, Paris whipped off her holiday chef's apron, smoothed the skirt of her dress and hurried to answer the door off the utility room that linked the house to the three-car garage.

"Cody. This is a surprise." Illuminated by the soft lantern light of the log home's rustic outdoor fixture, his hair shone a glossy black and emphasized the strong planes of his face. Alert brown eyes met hers and her heart beat a faster clip as she opened the door wider. "Please come in. It's cold out tonight."

"I'm here only long enough to drop this off." He nodded to the cardboard box in his arms.

"What is it? I'm not expecting a delivery." And certainly not from Cody.

"I was down at Dix's a short while ago and Sharon mentioned you'd called earlier today saying you needed this for tonight. But no one had come by to pick it up."

She stared at him blankly, noticing how his five o'clock shadow skimmed a firm jaw and his lips curved upward ever so slightly as if something amused him.

He raised a dark brow. "Ginger ale? For the punch?"

"Oh!" Paris gave a halfhearted laugh. "I totally forgot. What's that tell you about how this day has gone?"

"I imagine you've been busy, if that line of parked cars leading all the way down to the road is any indication. Your annual Christmas open house?"

"That's right."

So he remembered Mom and Dad always hosted one. It had been a gathering of family and close friends, the community's movers and shakers and those out-of-towners who'd done significant business with Perslow Real Estate and Property Management. The family of Leroy Hawk, of course, had never been invited.

"At your old place, Dad and I used to wrap the trees and porch railings with lights. Remember? We'd line the perimeter of the yard and driveway with luminarias and set up the crèche scene out front."

Suddenly she envisioned the handsome, well-built teenager working alongside his dad the weekend after Thanksgiving. She'd spied on him more than once from her upstairs window.

"It always looked beautiful. Mom loved it."

"She was a real kid about Christmas, wasn't she?"

"She was. She'd start listening to Christmas music in October while she planned the open house, made homemade decorations and tested out new recipes."

"Some of that rubbed off on you, too, as I recall." Cody's smiling gaze met hers at the shared memory. "I remember she used to invite neighborhood kids to sit on the porch with her while she read the Christmas story and gave out sugar cookies. You did that after she passed away. Do you still do it?"

She shook her head, a pang of melancholy touching her heart as she motioned to the treed property surrounding the isolated log home. "No. There are no neighbor kids out here."

"That's a shame." He shifted the box in his arms. "That's where I heard my first Bible stories as a kid, listening in while I helped Dad with the yard work."

Before he'd been hired full-time, Leroy Hawk had done odd jobs for the Perslows and others around town, often taking his son along when Cody wasn't in school. Sometimes it seemed, even when a young boy, that Cody did much of the work while his father wandered off for a cigarette or shot the breeze with another neighbor.

"Mom did love everything about the season," Paris continued as more memories surfaced. "Decorating the tree and fixing the food. Playing every Christmas tune she knew on the piano. Sledding and cross-country skiing. That was when I was pretty young though, before the MS got bad."

Cody's expression softened. "You still miss her, don't you?"

"I do." In many ways it seemed like only yesterday that Mom was here, yet at other times it seemed like forever since they'd last spoken, since they'd held each other. How she wished she could have her mother here now, to have grown their relationship into that of adult friends.

Abruptly aware of the chill swirling in around her ankles, she stepped back from the doorway. "I'm sorry. I've left you standing out in the cold."

"No problem. I'll set this inside the door—unless you want me to take it on in to wherever you want it." His dark eyes met hers in question.

Dad hadn't been happy when Elizabeth told him last night that Cody was helping with the Christmas gala and he might not be any happier to find Cody on the premises this evening. Through the open door behind her, she could hear Carrie and her friends chattering as they entered the kitchen. Hopefully the teen wouldn't carelessly voice aloud her disappointment in the good-looking "hired help."

"Right by the door would be fine."

He leaned in to set the box on the terra-cotta tiles, gave it a shove to the side, then stepped back.

"I hope your open house is a success." He glanced toward the car-lined drive, now deep in shadow except where illuminated by solar fixtures. Another cluster of chatting guests made its way up the gradual incline. "Looks like more arrivals are heading this way."

"It's fun seeing old friends and hosting Dad's clients."

"Enjoy." He nodded a farewell, then headed back down the drive.

"Cody?"

He turned almost expectantly. "Yeah?"

"Thank you for making the delivery." She took a quick breath. "And for remembering Mom."

He smiled that slow, lazy smile of his, his eyes filled with understanding. "Anytime."

Cody strode along the side of the dimly lit driveway, nodding to another knot of guests heading up to the log home. He didn't know any of them, but they smiled a warm greeting. His own thoughts weren't on the house party, though, but on how stunning Paris looked tonight. Her hair had been swept atop her head, a few loose tendrils gently framing her face. A simple, charcoal-gray dress and pearls at her neck set off her breathtaking beauty.

She said it was a surprise to see him, but if she thought it weird that he'd made the delivery, she hadn't said so. He'd stopped at Dix's at the end of the day when Sharon had taken notice of the forgotten carton on the counter. She'd picked up the phone to call Paris, but with only a moment's hesitation Cody volunteered to drop off the box, saying he imagined everyone at the Perslow's was caught up in party preparations.

The time he'd taken for the detour had been well worth it.

With a grin, he kicked a pinecone, sending it scuttling down the drive ahead of him. When it came to Paris he was still looking for ways to help her, to please her. To draw her admiring gaze.

Mentioning her mother hadn't been an intentional ploy to gain her favor. But she seemed to appreciate that someone fondly remembered Marna Perslow at Christmastime. It had to have been hard these fourteen years, a young girl prematurely cut off from the loving influence of a mother like hers.

"Hawk!"

Cody's attention jerked from his reverie, his senses on alert at the sharp tone of a male voice. The light strings wrapping the pine trunks cast spotty shadows along the dark, forested drive and it took a moment to identify the source of the voice that had halted him. Up ahead a man leaned casually against the door of Cody's truck.

Owen Fremont.

Great. Cody strode on toward him, determined not to let the puffed-up man cow him because he possessed money and social status—and the assumption that he'd netted Paris.

When he approached, Owen pushed himself away from the truck, but didn't extend a hand in greeting. "Leaving the party? The night's still young."

The query didn't deserve a response. Owen knew, if for no other reason than how Cody was dressed, that he hadn't been in attendance. Unknown to Owen, though, he'd spent the past decade mixing with business and social acquaintances of his friend Trevor's exceedingly well-off parents. Had he been invited tonight, he'd have held his own just fine. Offering explanation to this joker didn't set well, but he nevertheless answered politely enough. "I was making a delivery."

The other man nodded as if satisfied that Cody hadn't overstepped his bounds. "Fine people, the Perslows."

"They are."

"With an impeccable reputation."

"That, too."

Owen slid his hands into the pockets of his neatly pressed trousers and shrugged a topcoat-clad shoulder as he gave Cody a calculating look. "I don't see any point in beating around the bush, *Mister* Hawk."

Cody folded his arms. "Then let's hear it."

Owen gave a soft laugh. "I've done some checking around since Paris introduced us yesterday morning."

"And?"

"I have no doubt you already know what the reputation of a Hawk is like in this town."

"Why don't you tell me?"

Owen grinned. "I don't think that's necessary, do you? I'm not here to disparage your family. I'm certain there's little I can share that you aren't aware of."

"Well, then?"

Owen pinned Cody with a challenging look. "I merely want to bring it to your attention that Perslows and Hawks don't—how should I put this?—mix. And Paris—"

"You can leave Paris out of this."

"Oh, but we both know we can't, don't we? So I'm asking—as one *gentleman* to another—" even in the dim light, Cody didn't miss Owen's mocking smile "—that you keep in mind a woman's reputation in a small town can too easily be tarnished by even the most innocent behaviors on the part of, let's say, a man who admires her?"

This jerk was so full of himself it wasn't funny.

Cody stepped around him and opened the driver-side door to his truck. He climbed inside, then looked back at the smirking man who'd had the effrontery to warn him away from Paris. Owen must not be that confident of his own standing with her or he wouldn't try to run off perceived competition. Was he beginning to realize money couldn't buy everything, including a woman's heart?

"I'm relieved you're aware of that hazard of

small-town living, *Mister* Fremont," Cody said, his tone dry, "and that you intend to mind your manners around Miss Perslow."

Cody slammed the vehicle's door, started up the truck, then drove off without a backward glance.

Open her eyes, Lord. Soon.

Chapter Nine

"I can hardly believe that in less than two weeks I'll walk out of here as Mrs. Brett Marden." Abby Diaz sighed happily as she and Paris looked around the sanctuary of Canyon Springs Christian Church early Saturday morning. An overcast day, with little natural light illuminating the space, it was nevertheless cheerfully decorated for the season with greenery and red velvet bows. There wouldn't be much to do in that respect for the evening wedding except to light candles.

"Are you nervous, Abby? Even a little bit?"

Did other brides have nagging second thoughts? Or was she the only one who ever doubted she'd be the kind of wife her fiancé deserved?

"You mean am I getting cold feet? No way." Abby laughed and shook back her black hair. "I have absolute peace about marrying my cowboy."

Absolute peace. Paris hadn't had that as her own wedding day approached.

"So are we finished here?" Their meeting had taken longer than Paris anticipated and she was cutting it close for her next appointment. "We can stop by Kit's Lodge next week to review final details for catering the reception."

"Perfect," Abby pronounced, then cast Paris a sympathetic look. "But I know helping with my wedding has to be difficult for you. I'm sure that—"

"I'm thrilled to be helping you," Paris quickly cut in. She gave the bride a hug and, as soon as Abby departed, she returned to her own vehicle, disappointed that she wouldn't have time to swing by Pine Shadow Ridge and check on Cody's progress.

She glanced skyward at the slate-gray clouds, then headed in the direction of Main Street. It felt weird at times to be around a guy who'd declared his love a dozen years ago, when neither of them were much more than kids. Did he now find his youthful confession embarrassing or did he shrug it off? Was he relieved nothing had come of his adolescent declaration and that he hadn't been stuck with her for the past decade?

It had to have taken courage on his part to speak up those many years ago. Courage—or madness. They hadn't run with the same crowd in school. In fact, Cody didn't really run with any crowd. He'd been a loner. Did being around her now feel uncomfortable to him, too, remembering how she'd turned him away that night?

She wouldn't have dared do otherwise, of course,

no matter how her heart clamored for his kisses. Dad would have locked her in her room and she'd never have seen the light of day before she turned eighty. Thankfully, Cody seemed to prefer leaving that episode in the past. But it still felt strange. Awkward. And she couldn't help wondering what *would* have happened had he kissed her that night…

Shaking off the memories, she found a parking space not far from Dix's Woodland Warehouse.

"Sorry I'm late, Sharon," Paris called as she entered the store. She rounded a display of outdoor gear on her way to the office at the rear of the building, then drew to a halt.

Cody looked up from where he perused the contents of one of the shelves. "Good morning, Paris. You're starting your day early."

She willed her suddenly hammering heart to slow at this unexpected encounter with the very man she'd been thinking about.

"I just met with Abby Diaz at the church and now I'm here to see Sharon. The dress she'd ordered for her wedding fell through, but I think I've found something online that she'll like. It's in stock and available for express shipping."

"I'm a big advocate for shopping locally, but the internet can sure come through in a pinch."

"It can." She took a quick breath and offered a smile. "Thank you again for delivering the extra ginger ale last night. We did end up using most of it."

"I was happy to help."

When he'd departed, she'd regretted not insisting he come inside in spite of how her father might have felt about it. Not being dressed for the occasion, he may not have wanted to join the other guests, but he might have enjoyed sampling the appetizers in the kitchen and visiting with Carrie and her young cohorts. Who knows, maybe after spending time in his company Carrie would have regretted so quickly dismissing a Hawk as undesirable. Most people didn't realize how fortunate they were to be born into a well-respected family, not being forever judged due to negative familial associations.

As Paris was well aware, the past and people's preconceptions could be a heavy burden.

"I know why Paris is here," Sharon called as she came from the back of the store, "but is there something I can help you with, Cody?"

"I'm picking up refills for my staple gun." He reached for a box.

Sharon tilted her head in interest. "I heard you were taking over the Christmas gala decorating for your mother. An answered prayer—right, Paris?"

Paris's attention flickered to Cody. "I don't know what we'd do without him."

"He was a skilled craftsman, even as a teenager. I'd give about anything to have a work shed like the one he built for his mother."

"It's nothing fancy, Sharon." Cody dismissed her

comment with a shrug, but Paris could tell he was pleased by the compliment.

"You don't think so? The workspace and built-ins make it a hobbyist's dream." She nodded in Paris's direction. "You'll have to get him to show you."

Would he? He didn't look to be so inclined.

"With Cody in charge of the staging," Sharon added as she gave him an approving nod, "Bill and I are especially looking forward to this year's gala."

Cody caught Paris's eye, questioning what he thought he'd heard. Sharon and her fiancé would be attending the charity dinner and dance?

While both were established business owners in Canyon Springs, the holiday event had long been a gathering of the socially prominent moneyed elite of local townspeople and neighboring communities. It had been a private affair, not city-sponsored, an exclusive celebration as they bestowed their year-end tax deductible donations on behalf of the less fortunate. A tight-knit clique from what he remembered.

"You won't be disappointed," Paris assured Sharon. "Lucy's design is fabulous and it's apparent from what I've seen that Cody's rendering of it will be one to remember."

Sharon gave him a considering look. "Keep in mind, Cody, that Paris is gifted herself when it comes to bringing this type of thing to life. You might wield a mean hammer and saw, but don't hesitate to recruit her if you need help with the decorative details."

He again caught Paris's now-discomfited gaze, suspecting the last thing she needed was one more thing to do, and that doing anything with *him* would fall at the bottom of her wish list. He gave her an understanding smile. "I think she already has plenty on her plate this season."

"Not the least of which," Sharon admitted, her eyes now fixed on Paris, "is the added burden of helping those of us less adept with wedding prep-arations. Give me a few minutes to make a phone call, doll, then come on back and let's get that dress ordered and free up the rest of your day."

When Sharon disappeared into the office and shut the door, Paris turned to Cody with a pen-etrating look. "If I'm not mistaken, you seemed taken aback when Sharon said she'd be attending the gala."

"Sharon and Bill may be long-established resi-dents but not, shall we say, the crème de la crème of Canyon Springs society."

"They're well-thought-of."

"I'm not questioning that."

"But you are," she said evenly, "questioning how they'd fit in?"

He shrugged. "I'm wondering if they wouldn't find the event an uncomfortable one."

He could tell by the flash in her eyes that he'd

stumbled on *her* hot button. He should have kept his mouth shut.

She tilted her head, as if weighing her words.

"You know, Cody," she said softly, aware as he was, that they weren't alone in the store, "you're not going to like hearing this, but you're very judgmental. Did you know that? You're prejudiced against people you don't even know because they're better-off than you."

"Whoa, there." He drew back with a forced smile, keeping his own voice low. "Prejudiced? Judgmental? I think that's a little harsh, don't you?"

Paris leveled a troubled look at him. "No more harsh than you thinking that because someone has money and social standing that they are innately snobbish. That's as far from the truth as you can get."

"You think so?" A too-familiar bitterness welled up inside. "Try standing on a stage in your patched jeans and worn flannel shirt with a roomful of elegantly dressed strangers staring at you. Looking down on you while someone passes out token gifts to the town's 'needy' kids."

Paris opened her mouth to respond, but he cut her off. "Those gifts didn't make a dent in their wallets, didn't inconvenience them in the least. But they got a warm, fuzzy holiday feeling before heading back to their big fancy homes, thanking God they and theirs were more *deserving* of His blessings."

A flicker of pity flashed through Paris's eyes,

only to be quickly replaced with resolve. "I'm sorry you experienced that, Cody—or interpreted it that way. The committee no longer distributes gifts to kids at the gala itself. They haven't done that since you were a kid. But even when they did, you're mistaken about the spirit in which those gifts were given."

"Come on, Paris. You can't have been blind to it." She was too compassionate, too sensitive to have overlooked it.

"Are you saying my *mother* was like that? For years before her health prohibited it, she played an instrumental role in ensuring the gala was a successful fund-raising event." Paris's eyes darkened with emotion. "Do you think she looked down on those in need, on those who'd suffered from financial setbacks or from doing nothing more wicked than being born into the 'wrong' family? That she gave only so she might feel, as you put it, all warm and fuzzy?"

Cody glanced around the store to make sure no one was paying attention to them. Man, he'd opened a can of worms trying to get Paris to understand where he was coming from. She was taking everything he'd said the wrong way, twisting it around.

"Of course I don't think that of your mother." He kept his voice low. "You're taking this too personally. Out of context."

At the sound of bells jingling above the doorway

as another bevy of customers entered, she gave him a sharp look. "Am I?"

Before he could respond, she lifted that stubborn chin of hers and brushed past him, heading to the back office as the heels of her boots clicked sharply on the hardwood floor.

Hours later, anger and disappointment still welled up as Paris made her way down the festively decorated Main Street. Laden with packages and shopping bags, she wove her way among the smiling holiday shoppers, attempting to be thankful for the eye-opening conversation she'd had with Cody. How foolish she'd been for toying with the idea that he might still be interested in her. For having any interest in *him*.

She glanced at her watch. Noon. She'd better hurry or she'd be late to set things up for the two-o'clock tea at the church. Being so busy, she hadn't been her usual organized self. Cody's presence during this holiday season hadn't helped either, leaving her anxious and unfocused.

Whoever would have thought he'd harbor such thoughts of good people who had done so much for others? His youthful experiences were unfortunate, but to imply that her mother and others like her were pretentious and patronizing, condescendingly looking down their noses at those who were less well-off, was so unfair.

Mom believed she and Dad had been financially blessed so that they might bless others. How often had she told Paris and the gala committee that God had expectations of those to whom He'd given much—that they weren't to be containers of God's gifts but channels to others of His blessings.

And to resent that? To think ill of well-meaning people?

"Paris!"

She turned to a cheerful female voice, spying her best friend dodging cars in her dash across Main Street, her tumble of long blond hair flying behind her.

"Whew!" Delaney Marks laughed as she leaped to the safety of the sidewalk. "Where is this traffic coming from? This *is* Canyon Springs, isn't it? I didn't take a wrong turn?"

Paris laughed. "No, you didn't get lost. You're really home for the holidays."

"I was worried there for a moment."

"When did you get back?" Her friend hadn't been in town for months.

"Yesterday."

"And you didn't call me? Didn't come to our open house?"

"I had other obligations last night. But I'm here now. Should we stop in for hot cocoa and a chat-fest at Camilla's?"

"I wish I could." Paris nodded to the packages in her arms and the shopping bag handles looped in the crooks of her elbows. "But I have to get this stuff to the church. The ladies' Christmas tea is this afternoon and I want to make sure everything's ready. Are you going to it?"

"No. But…" Delaney leaned in close, her voice a soft hiss in Paris's ear. "Don't think you can slip away without telling me about *him*."

Paris drew back. Even as teens, she'd never divulged her feelings for Cody to her friend. "Him who?"

Delaney's voice remained low, her eyes dancing with mischief. "You know…Cody Hawk."

"Believe me," Paris said, her face warming as she pulled away from her friend and started off down the street once again, "there's nothing to tell."

Except that she'd been stupid for thinking that he might still have a thing for her, and that with the passage of time they could bridge the differences in their upbringings, which had separated them as teens.

Delaney quickly caught up with her. "Nothing to tell? That's not what I'm hearing."

Dismayed, Paris halted. "What are you hearing?"

"Not just hearing. But seeing." Delaney fanned her hand in front of her face as if she might swoon right then and there. "Oh. My. Goodness. He is one hunky guy."

"You've seen him?"

"Yeah, coming out of Dix's earlier this morning. Jacquie pointed him out. No wonder you're willing to risk stepping over to the other side of the tracks."

"Who says I'm doing that?" Maybe she *had* been contemplating the idea, but not after that run-in with Cody a few hours ago.

"Kirsten mentioned it. Jacquie, too. Of course, they're claiming to be concerned that you're dishonoring Dalton's memory, risking tarnishing your reputation. But personally, I think they're just jealous."

"There's nothing to be jealous of."

Delaney cast her a disbelieving look. "Kirsten says he was seen slinking away from a side door at your place last night and that you've been rendezvousing with him at Pine Shadow Ridge."

Small towns. Paris gritted her teeth as she juggled the packages in her arms. Dropped one. Delaney picked it up and handed it to her.

"Cody made a delivery for the open house and he's helping his mother with the Christmas gala decorations. Since you've obviously caught up on the local gossip, surely you've also heard she can't do it herself because his father had a stroke?"

"Yep." Delaney grimaced. "Brought on by alcohol abuse and a lottery ticket bust."

Amazing. Her friend had barely been in town twenty-four hours and she had the scoop on everything, even if the piece about Cody was distorted.

"So, Paris..." Delaney looked furtively around them, her eyes again twinkling. She could be so lovable—and exasperating. "Is he a good kisser?"

Her breath caught unexpectedly at the prospect

of Cody's warm mouth on hers. Aware from the heat rising up her neck that her face was probably crimson, she swatted playfully at her friend.

And sent the armful of packages tumbling in all directions.

She groaned.

"Could you use some help?" a familiar male voice called from behind her.

Dread mingling with an inexplicable lifting of her spirits, she turned to see Cody striding across the street toward her.

Chapter Ten

Paris didn't look overjoyed to see him. But no matter. He had an apology to make and there was no time like the present.

Cody crouched at her booted feet and gathered the scattered packages into his arms. Then he stood, looking down into her apprehensive gray eyes. After their misunderstanding this morning, he wasn't surprised at not receiving a warm welcome. But their earlier conversation had been an overdue wake-up call for him. As much as he'd like to believe that the past twelve years lessened the impact their different backgrounds made on their lives, that theory had proven to be untrue.

"Thank you, Cody."

She reached for his armload, but he gripped it more tightly. "Where are you heading with this? To your car?"

"Yes, but—"

"Where's it at?"

He glanced around for the SUV, suddenly becoming aware of a cute blonde woman off to the side looking up at him with open amusement. Was she going to stand there and stare at him or go on about her business? He had something he needed to say to Paris and didn't want bystanders eavesdropping.

"There it is, Cody," the blonde said, standing on her tiptoes to point to a spot over his right shoulder and down the street.

He frowned. She knew him? Did he know her?

"Uh, thanks." He glanced at a rosy-cheeked Paris who motioned to the other woman.

"Cody, this is my friend Delaney Marks. She moved here shortly after you left town. Delaney, this is Cody Hawk."

Good. He didn't know her so there would be no expectation of catching up on old times with someone who'd stuffed him in a box of preconceptions labeled "loser."

But he still needed to be alone with Paris.

"Nice to meet you, Delaney." He'd offer his hand to her but couldn't risk scattering the packages once again.

She beamed up at him. "And it's *wonderful* to meet you."

Wonderful?

Paris cut her friend a sharp look, then turned to him. "If you're sure you wouldn't mind…" She motioned in the direction of her vehicle.

"Lead the way."

He followed, looking back only once to see the Delaney gal still rooted in place, thankfully not inclined to join them. Catching his eye, she wiggled her fingers in a merry wave. Blew him a kiss.

Flirty little minx. He squared his shoulders and focused again on Paris as, shopping bags looped over her arms, she made her way to her SUV. When they reached it, she lifted the tailgate, placed her bags inside and then stepped back to give him room to do likewise. He took his time divesting himself of his burden, taking care to arrange the packages where they wouldn't tip or slide.

"Looks like that does it." He stepped back and lowered the tailgate, checking to make certain it latched securely.

Her gaze met his uncertainly. "Thank you, Cody."

"You're more than welcome." He cut a glance back to the spot from which they'd come, confirming there was no sign of the blonde. Then he leaned a hand against the edge of the SUV's roof. "I guess we got off to a bad start this morning."

Paris smiled faintly, shaking her head. "Let's not revisit it, okay?"

"I'm not intending to revisit it. I want to apologize." He ran his thumb along the door window's chrome, gathering his thoughts. "I didn't mean to imply your mother—or any of the others—operated out of selfish motives with their charity work.

The annual Christmas gala funds many critical projects throughout the year."

"Yes, it does."

He cleared his throat. "I had no right to say the things I said. I'm sorry, Paris. I hope you can forgive me."

"You only said what you thought."

"What a *kid* thought." His eyes narrowed. "A kid whose worthless dad was always pushing him forward to get whatever he could from those who were willing to share from their own abundance. A kid who'd been humiliated time and time again in front of adults and his peers as he lined up for freebies."

Her gaze softened. "I know that couldn't have been easy."

He glanced down the street, then caught her eye again. "Do you remember the year I was a junior— you were a freshman—when you and your Dad distributed food boxes? You gave one to me."

She nodded slightly, her expression solemn at the recollection. He remembered it like yesterday.

"I had a big fight with Dad before I went that afternoon," he continued, forcing away the memory of a blush that had tinged Paris's cheeks when her startled gaze met his that day. "He told me if I didn't go, I could forget about coming home. Ever."

A soft whimper escaped her lips. "Oh, Cody—"

He held up his hand to stay her words. He wasn't looking for sympathy. He wanted her to understand why he'd said—stupidly said—the words he'd uttered that morning.

"When I saw you there with your dad, with a few of our classmates, I wanted to die on the spot. I was so ashamed. Dad had a job. I was working when I could. We had food and clothes—or we would have if he didn't periodically drink it all away."

He took a deep breath and let it out slowly. "After we talked this morning, I went back to the project and hammered out my anger on that poor defenseless wood." He gave a halfhearted chuckle. "In the process I came to realize what you heard this morning was a mortified kid's way of coping. And…I'm sorry, Paris."

Their gazes held for a long moment, the hustle and bustle of shoppers fading away as he focused on her.

"It's okay," she said quietly. "I should apologize, as well. I shouldn't have—"

"No. You had every right to say what you'd said. I never intended to slander good people who help others in need. I was wrong."

She didn't respond, a sadness in her eyes. *Pity?* Once again he felt as he had that day when she'd handed him the food box. He fisted his fingers and lightly rapped the top of her vehicle.

"So, that's it. All I have to say."

And without bringing himself to look at her again, he turned away and strode back across the street.

* * *

When she left the church late that afternoon following cleanup of the ladies' tea, Paris ignored the chiming of her cell phone except to confirm the caller ID. It was Delaney, no doubt wondering what conversation had ensued with Cody.

She wasn't ready to talk about it with anyone. Not even her best friend.

Throughout the long afternoon of pouring tea and serving holiday cookies, her mind had drifted to him repeatedly. Not only to the Cody who'd stood apologetically before her earlier that afternoon, but to the Cody she'd known through the years.

The Cody who'd been among a handful of boys roughhousing on the playground, but who had been the only one singled out to be sent to the principal's office.

The Cody who'd been made fun of when he'd come to school in a too-small coat and who subsequently chose for the remainder of the winter to brave the cold with only a knit cap, scarf and gloves.

The Cody who'd missed out on participating in school sports he probably would have excelled at, maybe would have received a college scholarship for, had he not been working alongside his dad when he wasn't in class.

In many ways, through no fault of his own, his life had been an uphill battle.

Now upstairs in her room, she stepped into her walk-in closet and lifted a fabric-covered box from a shelf. It was in the roomy container that she kept the treasures nearest and dearest to her heart. A photo of Mom and Dad on their wedding day lay on top. Below that snuggled a small cedar box containing, among other things, her first wristwatch, class ring and the sparkling chandelier earrings Mom loved to wear at the holidays. Below lay a leather-bound journal. She'd never kept a diary, but she'd written poetry. Opening the book, she removed a piece of paper tucked between the pages and carefully unfolded it to reveal a pen-and-ink portrait.

Gazing down at the girl she once was, she vividly remembered the beautiful autumn day Cody had run to catch up with her as she walked home from the high school. He'd startled her when, eyes dark and attentive, he'd carefully torn the sketch from his newsprint pad and handed it to her.

"For you," he'd said, his voice low. Almost gruff. "You can keep it if you want to."

Looking down at it, then back up at him, their gazes had locked for a heart-stopping moment. She'd been embarrassed. Thrilled. Unable to breathe. Incapable of saying anything more than thank you, she'd broken their too-intimate visual connection and hurried the rest of the way home. She didn't dare look back.

Although they'd later seen each other at school, they didn't speak more than a few words until that night a year and a half later when he'd shown up on her doorstep. But she'd thought of him often. Dreamed of him. Prayed for him.

She ran her finger across the still-dark ink of the sketch, gently refolded it and slipped it back into the journal. Then she turned to the pages where, in her own distinctive cursive she'd penned one of many free-verse poems she'd composed during her adolescent years. More than one written with Cody in mind.

I look at you sometimes...
And wish I could read your voice.
Or better still, your smile.
So gentle, tender and quick to please,
Most Sweet, I feel awed when you bestow it
on me.
I belong to you and am thus honored—
Or could it be only my imagination?
I look at you sometimes
And I wish...

Paris quickly closed the journal and returned it to the box. Then, with a weary sigh, she leaned back on the pillows propped against the headboard of her bed and closed her eyes as the day faded into twilight.

Delaney said people were talking about them. Making wrong assumptions. Cody was helping with the Christmas gala, that was all. How could they construe that as dishonoring Dalton's memory?

Anger sparked. Did this town expect her to never find someone else to love? Was she to be permanently bound to her dead fiancé? Or even worse, did they expect her to settle for someone who she had little in common with beyond their single status and the level of their family finances and social standing?

But what those who criticized an innocent relationship with Cody didn't understand was that, even if she threw caution to the wind and took up with the former "bad boy"—*if* he would have her—she didn't deserve his love, a home, a family. Hadn't her selfishness ensured Dalton would never see his own dreams fulfilled?

"Lord," she whispered, the ache in her heart weighing heavily, "I'm coming to care for Cody, but what am I supposed to do?"

Chapter Eleven

He hadn't seen Paris since Saturday, when he'd helped her load her vehicle and apologized for his regrettable outburst. But that was just as well. He needed to focus on the job at hand, and an uninterrupted dawn-to-dark day on Monday and most of today had given him a huge leap in progress. If all went well, he'd be working on the cabin roofs by noon.

Sunday, naturally, had been spent with Ma, and another brief visit with his father. The ministrokes Dad had suffered in the weeks since the major one continued. He'd rally one day, then seem to lose ground the next. It wasn't looking good and, in spite of Cody's conflicted feelings about his father, his heart ached for his mother.

Unexpectedly, though, as the days passed since his return to Canyon Springs, less and less Cody felt the need to press his father to right the wrongs done to his son. Felt less the need to demand an apology, to hear him admit his mistakes and ask forgiveness. Cody recognized that wasn't likely to happen, and the issue God pressed upon him wasn't one of his father's responsibility, but of his own.

Extending forgiveness when it wasn't asked for wasn't only to absolve the one who'd done the wrong but to free the one who'd been wronged.

Cody pulled the filtering mask over his mouth and nose, adjusted his goggles and angled the free-standing light for better illumination. Then he finished spray painting the base color for the tubing "logs." He noted with satisfaction that the spackle underneath the grayish-brown gave off an even better woodlike effect than he'd originally hoped.

"You've sure been putting in long hours," Jim Harper said as he stopped by to inspect Cody's work. He often paused to chat a few minutes when he came in the maintenance building for the workday ahead. "Looks like this year's gala is going to be impressive."

Cody paused and pulled the filter down to dangle around his neck. "Are you going?"

Jim snorted. "Are you kidding me? What would I be doing hobnobbing with the town's elite? Are *you?*"

"No plans to." In fact, it hadn't even crossed his mind. Even if the gala was no longer strictly a high society event, tickets wouldn't be cheap and would have sold out months ago.

"Come on, Hawk. You mean Paris doesn't have

you measured for a penguin suit and your shoes polished to a glossy shine?"

Cody shrugged off the good-natured teasing with a grin. "I'm glad you're deriving some amusement from this, Jim."

His friend slapped him on the back. "Much appreciated, pal. Much appreciated."

With another laugh his former classmate headed off and Cody pulled on the filter once again. No, he wouldn't be going to the charity event and he hadn't heard Ma mention attending, either. But surely she'd been invited, hadn't she? Regardless, he'd slip her over here once the clubhouse was decked out in its finery. Although she'd teased him about overseeing his work, she hadn't yet come by to take a peek at his progress.

The remainder of the day flew by and he had a good running start on the cabin roofs before finally calling it quits at close to eight o'clock. It had snowed this evening—maybe three or four inches—and was still coming down. He needed to get back to Ma's, get some supper and give his business partner a call.

He stepped into the parking lot and firmly pulled the auto-locking door closed behind him when a blinding glare halted him in his tracks. He turned his head slightly to the side and lifted his forearm to shade his eyes, attempting to make out the vehicle that had pinned him with its piercing lights.

Irritated, he waved them away with his free arm. "Hey, knock it off!"

The lights abruptly shut off, but his eyes were still adjusting when he heard the sound of the vehicle's door open and saw a shadowy figure step out. The door closed again.

"Sorry about that, Hawk."

Merle Perslow, if he wasn't mistaken. But the scornful tone of his voice belied the apology and Cody didn't make any attempt to respond to the mocking words.

"So, you think you'll make the deadline?" The man approached, now visible in the faint pool of light provided by the door's overhead fixture. He halted a few yards away from Cody.

"I see no reason why not."

Paris's father gave a cursory glance around the parking lot. "I can think of a few myself."

"Sir?"

Merle tilted his head, eyeing Cody. "You'd be further along if you focused on the work at hand and limited your distractions."

Cody took a slow breath. "With my father in the hospital and my mother in need of assistance, I'm giving as much time to the project as I can. I'm confident things will meet the committee's expectations."

"Your efforts to help your family are commendable. But we both know that isn't the distraction I'm referring to."

Paris.

Merle's brows lowered. "I thought on the day you came to see me about the status of your father's employment that we'd come to a mutual agreement."

Cody met the belligerent gaze with a blandly innocent one. "There were strings attached to those concessions?"

"Cody, Cody, Cody." Merle gave a bitter chuckle. "You haven't changed since you were a teenager, have you? You still have your eye on a grand prize you're not even in the running for."

Is that how he saw his daughter? A prize to be awarded to a man who fit his idea of who and what Paris needed in her life? Nevertheless, Merle's casual dismissal of him stung, as if being brushed away like an annoying gnat.

"I agreed to fulfill my mother's contract and that's what I intend to do," Cody said quietly, having no intention of getting tangled up in a confrontation with this man. He was Paris's father and for that reason alone he'd show him respect.

Merle smirked. "That was a convenient windfall for you, wasn't it? You know, with your mother reneging on her contractual obligations."

Cody tensed at the inferred slur on his mother's integrity.

"Surely you can't believe Dad's stroke was deliberately timed to release her from her responsibilities."

"Of course not. But…" Merle raked his hand

through his neatly groomed hair, then he fixed a challenging glare on Cody. "Look, let's stop dodging the issue here. You're seeing more of my daughter than is required to get this job done. I want that to stop."

"I've rarely seen your daughter."

Merle's mouth twisted into a grimace. "That's not what I'm hearing."

So Owen Fremont had gotten in his two cents' worth? What better tactic than to manipulate Paris's father into running off the competition.

"I'm speaking the truth, Mr. Perslow."

"Truth?" Merle snorted. "That's a foreign language for a Hawk, wouldn't you say?"

Cody managed a shrug, keeping his temper in check. Unlike in his younger days, he wouldn't give Mr. Perslow the satisfaction of getting him riled. "So you've come here to tell me you've rethought your position on Dad's situation?"

Merle waved him away, his expression darkening. "We both know your father's 'situation' is immaterial. I'm here to make it clear there's only so much I'll take of the games Hawks play. You got that?"

Without waiting for a response, Merle leveled a final glare, then swung around to march back to his SUV, snow crunching under his boots.

Fists clenched, Cody watched in seething silence as the arrogant man climbed into the Lexus. This time Cody didn't flinch when the headlights again hit him. But when the engine gunned to roaring life and the vehicle lurched forward, his muscles tensed as he prepared to make a running leap into the nearby stand of ponderosas.

But the SUV only made a tight circle, then headed out of the parking lot, the glow of its tail-lights illuminating the still-falling snow.

"Look out, Paris!" The warning was accompanied by a feminine squeal of laughter as a snowball smacked into the windshield she was endeavoring to clean off.

Paris bent to scoop up a handful of snow from the church parking lot and packed it tight in her gloved hands. Then, attempting to keep her balance on the frosty surface, she sent the frozen missile sailing over the SUV's roof to the vehicle next to her. Missed.

"You throw like a girl!" Delaney taunted as she ducked into her car and pulled the door shut. Then she started the engine, flipped on the lights and made a face at Paris out the driver-side window as she negotiated her car from its parking spot.

"Isn't it great to have Delaney back?" Kara Kenton called from where she was scraping ice and snow from her rear window. Snow was falling faster than they could clean it off their vehicles.

"Oh, yeah, great." Laughing, Paris brushed the frozen crystals from the front of her jacket. Her friend had a more accurate aim than Paris could ever hope to have.

"We'll gang up on her soon," promised Olivia McGuire as she climbed into her own vehicle. "Drive carefully, ladies. I just got a call from Rob and he says it's slick out there."

"Where are the men in our lives when we need them?" Kara pouted aloud and a half dozen women scattered throughout the parking lot responded with their own laughing protests. Everyone was in high spirits after Abby Diaz's bridal shower. Her fiancé had gallantly picked her up afterward and most of the guests had also departed, but a number of the women had stayed to clean the church's kitchen and fellowship hall. Unfortunately, another snow squall moved through as they worked, depositing a fresh, frosty layer.

Paris used her snowbrush to again swipe at her windows, noticing that a pickup truck was slowing to a crawl on the street parallel to where she stood. Recognition dawned and before she could stop herself, she waved.

Cody.

To her surprise, he pulled into the parking lot—or rather slid in—and came to a halt not far from her. The next thing she knew, he'd bounded out of the truck with a long-handled, heavy-duty snowbrush and ice scraper combo. Booted feet wide apart and slowly raising the metal-handled, retractable device over his head as if it were a massive barbell, he gazed around the parking lot.

All eyes were riveted on him and Paris couldn't help but smile. Tall, handsome and broad-shouldered with snowflakes lighting in his glossy black hair, he looked as if he could take on the world.

"So, ladies!" he called out in that low, yummy voice of his, a grin broadening, "whose car is first?"

A chorus of feminine cheers ensued as he was enthusiastically waved forward. In no time at all, he'd removed the snow from a handful of vehicles, cleaning off even the hard-to-reach tops of the SUVs. One by one the smiling ladies departed, waving happily.

And then, at long last, he turned to her.

She hadn't seen him since Saturday, hadn't dared let herself stop by Pine Shadow Ridge to check on his progress. Touched by his willingness to apologize, she was nevertheless still confused about how she felt about him, and decided avoidance was the most sensible route to go. He'd only be in town a short while longer. There was no reason to get tied in knots attempting to find answers to questions that were better left unasked.

He approached her slowly, almost warily, probably feeling as self-conscious as she did. Their last encounter had ended awkwardly. In fact, their last two meetings had ended on a less-than-comfortable note.

"I think you made a few fans tonight," she said,

injecting a lightness into her tone. He laughed and the sound sent a delicious warmth flowing through her veins.

"Never hurts to have fans." He fiddled with the snowbrush, pulling the handle to its maximum length. Then he methodically pushed the snow from the top of her vehicle off the far side as he'd done for the other ladies.

"How are things coming on the project?" she ventured.

"The cabins are painted down to the details and frosted plexiglass windows inserted so light coming in from behind will give the illusion of an interior aglow." He gave the heavy snow on top another push, making it look easier than she knew it to be. "I'm working on the shingled roofs now."

"The trees are scheduled to be delivered next Monday."

"Live trees, with burlap-wrapped bases, right?"

"Just like in your mom's design." She tucked her snowbrush under her arm and thrust her chilled hands into her pockets. "We have door prizes—attach a tag under plates on each table and, depending on where people sit, they win anything from the centerpiece to a wreath to a tree to take home to plant in their yard. There's no point in the decorations going to waste."

He cut her an amused look. "Do you think anyone wants to win one of a dozen faux cabins?"

Paris smiled. "You might be surprised. As sturdy

as you're building them, they may make clever holiday yard ornaments. Or the committee may choose to put them in storage for use again another year."

"I could see your mother setting them up as an entire woodland village in her front yard."

Surprised, she gazed up at him. "That sounds exactly like what she'd do."

He gave the snow another shove. "I liked your mom, Paris. I felt really bad when she died. I don't think I ever got the chance to tell you that."

Tears unexpectedly pricked her eyes and she again pulled out her snowbrush and swiped halfheartedly at one of the windows before placing the brush on the hood of her SUV. She missed Mom more than ever at this time of year. "You know, it's funny, but the night before she died…"

She'd never told anyone this. Why was she bringing it up now? Cody turned to give her a nod, encouraging her to continue.

"I dreamed…" She couldn't help but smile at the memory. "I dreamed Mom and I were walking in the forest with Dad. It was a beautiful snowy day with big fat fluffy flakes coming down around us. Mom was laughing and *dancing* around in the snow. Can you believe it? Twirling with her arms outstretched like a little kid."

Paris laughed and stretched out her own arms, marveling at the still-vivid dream.

"That sounds like a good dream to me," Cody said softly. "One worth remembering."

"It was, it really was. But then, all of sudden…" She swallowed, determined not to cry. "All of a sudden in the dream I realized that Mom wasn't in a wheelchair anymore. She wasn't using a walker or a cane. I grabbed Dad by the arm. Pulled him close and whispered, '*Look,* Dad.'"

Her voice broke as a single tear slid down her cheek and Cody set the snowbrush aside to reach for her hand.

She drew strength from the gentle grip with which he held her. "I…I said, 'Look, Dad. She's okay now. She's okay.' And it was like the happiest day of my life."

Her eyes sought Cody's compassion-filled ones.

"And then I woke up." She shook her head slowly. "I prayed it was a sign God would heal her, that we'd have a miracle."

"But it wasn't to be," he said, his voice gentle.

"No. That afternoon…Mom died."

"I'm sorry, Paris." Cody's voice came in a ragged breath as he opened his arms to her.

Chapter Twelve

What was he thinking? Her father all but threatened him with bodily harm if he didn't stay away from his daughter. Yet here he was, standing under the church's parking lot lights for God and the whole world to see, holding her as if he'd never let her go.

He shifted his arms more securely around her, savoring the scent of her as he placed his cheek against her soft hair. He didn't get a sense that she was crying, that there was a need to dry tears, but only that she sought a reassuring comfort of strong arms around her.

His arms. Not Owen Fremont's.

How many years had he dreamed of holding her this way?

"That dream?" she said softly, her voice muffled against his jacket, for she'd slipped her arms around him in response to his own embrace.

"What about it?" he whispered.

"It was God's gift to me, don't you think? To remind me there will come a day when Dad and I *will* laugh together with Mom in the presence of God."

"You will."

"Jesus promises He'll dry every tear and there will be no pain or mourning or death."

"No debilitating MS."

"No. No more." She pulled back slightly to look into his eyes. "How do people live without that promise, Cody? Without the reassurance God gives to get us through the loss, the pain?"

His chest tightened as he looked down at her, into her dewy eyes. At her sweet, kissable mouth. But now wasn't the time or place to be thinking thoughts like that. With effort, he lifted his gaze to the cascade of snowflakes coming down from above.

"It's not a way I'd choose to live now, apart from Him. I did for way too long, certain I had all the answers. That I had life figured out and it didn't include God."

"I'm glad you let Him find you, Cody. I know it must have been hard to recognize the love of a Heavenly Father when your only example of fatherhood was—"

"Leroy Hawk?"

Contrite eyes met his. "I'm sorry, I didn't mean—"

He placed a gloved finger to still her lips. "No, it's true. For the longest time the last thing I wanted was anyone in my life who called himself father, heavenly or not."

Should he tell her what the turning point had been? What had pushed him into God's welcoming embrace? The crust of his hard, rebellious heart had finally broken open when he'd learned of her engagement to Dalton Herrington III.

But he didn't want to remind her of Dalton. Not now. Not when he was holding her close.

As if only now becoming aware of how she pressed against him, she stepped back, a self-conscious, apologetic smile playing on her lips. Reluctantly he released her and the cold night air rushed in to replace the warm place she'd filled, both in his arms and in his heart.

"Thank you, Cody," she said, ducking her head almost shyly. "For listening. When you said you liked my mother, I—"

She motioned helplessly.

"I did like your mother." And he cared for her daughter even more.

"I guess I'd better get going before Dad places a call to search and rescue."

Her heading home might not be a half-bad idea. He sure didn't want Mr. Perslow looking for her and finding them here together. Despite the dismissive comment about his father's situation being "immaterial," he didn't trust her father not to renege on his agreement as he seemed to think Cody had.

"Maybe I should follow you, make sure you get there safely."

"Thank you, but…"

She took another step back, obviously now embarrassed for breaking down in front of him, clinging to him. Time had passed since they were teens, but not much else had changed. In the eyes of many, including Paris and her father, he remained the bad boy to her good girl. What is it he'd brazenly announced to her the night she'd turned him away? That one day she'd beg him to marry her?

No, he didn't see that happening. Ever.

"Why don't you pop inside and get your car warmed up?" he suggested. They'd stood there so long, another layer of white had settled on the windows from stem to stern. "Get the defroster going while I give your windows a final cleaning."

All too soon, he had her windows cleared, ever conscious that she was watching him from inside the warmth of her vehicle and thinking about… what?

Him?

She rolled down her window, snowflakes lightly catching in her dark hair. Her luminous eyes met his. "Thank you again, Cody. For everything."

And then, as always, she was gone.

What had gotten into her last night? And what must Cody think of how she'd behaved, wrapping her arms around him and holding on for dear life?

She was glad he didn't have any idea what was going through her mind as she looked up into his compassion-filled eyes, at his firm, inviting lips.

Or at least she hoped he didn't have any idea.

Could he feel her heart pounding as she'd pressed against him? Did he sense her confusion in those vulnerable few seconds when she'd drawn back from him after having poured out her heart about the dream?

But how good it had felt to be held in the security of his arms. What would it be like to be embraced like that for a lifetime? Knowing that someone was there for you no matter what, that they had your best in mind?

Someone like Cody.

She made her way through the snow outside the maintenance building at Pine Shadow Ridge shortly after noon, clutching a holiday-trimmed insulated box in her gloved hands. Turkey sandwiches with brie and cranberries, fresh and hot from Camilla's Café. Homemade sweet-potato chips.

She'd taken the afternoon off, but after last night should she be here, dropping in on Cody like this? At Abby's bridal shower, Sharon Dixon mentioned he'd confided the need for assistance in the making of pinecone wreaths and, well, she could assist as easily as the next person, right?

But as Delaney had pointed out, people were beginning to talk about her and Cody, even though there was nothing to talk about. Neither of them had done anything that could remotely be considered out of line. And even though as a teenager he'd professed his undying love, he hadn't given any hint that he still cared for her, hadn't taken advantage of her vulnerable state last night as many men would have done.

But it was probably getting around that he'd come to everyone's aid at the church—and that the two of them had been the last ones in the parking lot when the others departed.

She glanced back at her SUV. Should she leave the sandwiches by the door, drive away and then call to let him know she'd dropped them off?

But she'd no more thought of that alternative when the steel door opened and Jim Harper stepped out. His eyes brightened as he gave her a friendly nod and held the door open for her. "Good afternoon, Miss Perslow."

He eyed her and the insulated box with interest.

"Hello, Jim. Would you mind—?"

She started to hand off the box to him, but he leaned back in the open door.

"Hey, Hawk!" he hollered loud enough to wake the dead. "Special delivery. *Real* special."

Paris's cheeks warmed as Jim swept her a low bow and motioned her inside. The door closed behind her and, as her eyes adjusted to the interior's relative dimness, she saw Cody approaching, a puzzled look on his handsome face.

"Hello, Paris. What brings you out here?"

He sounded surprised, but not particularly pleased. Had he thought that by her forward behavior last night she was playing games with him?

"Sharon said you could use help with the pinecone wreaths. That's something I can do." She held out the insulated box, suddenly questioning why she'd thought to make such a personal overture as bringing him a meal. "And I thought…you might be hungry and would enjoy something hot for lunch."

He ran a hand through his hair, uncertainty flickering through his eyes. Obviously he didn't know what to make of her offer to help or the noontime delivery.

"Or," she said quickly, "you could save it for your dinner tonight."

He accepted the box. "No, no, lunch sounds great. Thanks."

She peered around him to the well-lit area in the far corner of the building. A small army of faux cabins lined the walls. "Maybe while you eat, you could get me started working on the wreaths? I have the afternoon off."

He grimaced. "I wish I'd known you were coming. Unfortunately, the frames, glue guns and supply of dried pinecones are at my folks' place."

"I guess I should have said something last night." But cradled in his arms, she hadn't been thinking of pinecone wreaths. "Do you have anything else I could do?"

Nice going, Paris. You're practically begging him

to find you a reason to stay while he consumes the meal you forced on him. He probably hates brie. And cranberries.

He glanced back at the work area. "Maybe I can find something…"

"Don't worry about it, okay? I didn't mean to interrupt your work. I thought, from what Sharon said, that there would be something I could do. It's been awhile, but Mom and I used to make pinecone wreaths together."

He tilted his head. "I remember that."

"You do?"

"Yeah. Dad and I'd come the weekend after Thanksgiving to set up the lights and lawn ornaments. Your mother invited us inside for cocoa and cookies. You both had your hair in ponytails tied with metallic gold ribbons, and pinecones spread across the kitchen table."

Paris laughed. "That's right. I'd forgotten."

She didn't think there was a single encounter with Cody she didn't remember. Yet here was one he recalled right down to the details.

He looked at the box still clutched in his hand. "You know, I could sure use someone who is wreath-savvy right about now. I hate losing the opportunity to make use of your time and talents when you're available."

"Could we go get the pinecones and the rest of the stuff? Then we could come back here and I could get to work."

He rubbed his free hand along the back of his neck and she abruptly realized she'd basically invited herself to his folks' place. Sharon mentioned last night that it was in a state of disrepair, so he probably wouldn't care to have visitors even if only long enough to pick up pinecones.

He shook his head. "This isn't the most comfortable place for doing that kind of work. Even with that space heater back there, it's cold. Drafty. I don't want you catching a chill at Christmas."

"I may not be Laura Ingalls Wilder," she teased, suddenly wanting to convince him she was up to the challenge, "but I do come from sturdy pioneer stock."

A smile quirked as he gave her an appreciative head-to-toe evaluation that sent the blood in her veins thrumming.

"What about..." Cody studied her thoughtfully. "Ma will be home early this afternoon. She has business in town to take care of so she's cutting her hospital visit short. We could head over to her place and recruit her for pointers. It's been awhile since I've made wreaths, so I could use a refresher."

"I could, too." She'd never been to Cody's parents' place and, in fact, was surprised he'd taken her suggestion to retrieve the supplies a step further. "I can drive while you eat."

His forehead wrinkled. "It might be better if we both took our own vehicles. That way neither of us has to come back here if we don't need to."

Plus, it might not be wise to be seen riding around town together. That would definitely feed the gossip mill.

"Are you sure you have time?" She felt as if her arrival had disrupted his plans for the day.

He shrugged. "It will be a good break and I really could use the help."

Thirty minutes later, Cody having consumed his lunch as he put away his tools, they headed out. She followed his truck to the outskirts of their community.

The neighborhood the Hawks lived in was one she'd rarely passed through. Its winding, graveled road wove through the towering trees among a hodgepodge of modest—and sometimes rundown—frame homes and trailers. Here and there beribboned wreaths or a plastic holiday yard ornament reminded that Christmas came to this part of town, too. When Cody pulled into the driveway of a double-wide trailer, she followed close behind.

He approached to hold open her door. "Let's grab pinecones from Ma's stash and find us a place at the kitchen table."

"Sounds good."

Together they walked through the snow to the back of the property where Paris was surprised to see the shed Cody had built wasn't a stark shelter for lawn mowers and garden hoses, but a cute wood-framed structure. Painted a creamy yellow, it boasted glass windows with white shutters and window boxes to showcase flowers in the summer months.

"This is adorable, Cody. No wonder Sharon wishes she had one, too."

"You like it?"

"I love it."

He looked pleased. "Ma needed a place to call her own, a place to work on her craft projects and gardening. Dad later put in electricity and heat for her."

"You're a talented man, do you know that?"

"Thanks." He reached for the doorknob and opened it wide to reveal a shadowed interior.

She eagerly stepped forward. "Oh, Cody, this is—"

An unexpected sound of movement from inside cut her words short and Cody protectively reached out to halt her.

She looked up at him uncertainly, her voice a whisper. "Do your parents have a dog?"

Frowning, he shook his head. "Maybe it's a mouse or squirrel."

They listened intently. Then the sound of movement came again, the scraping of something on the concrete floor. Not at all animal-like.

"Who's in there?" Cody called in a tone intended to intimidate.

No response.

"Ma should keep the door padlocked," he muttered under his breath, then stepped closer to the open doorway. "Whoever you are, come on out of there and show yourself!"

A rustling, crunching sound came from a far corner, outside their line of vision.

Cody nodded to Paris to step away from the door, then he again raised his voice. "I *said*—"

"Don't shoot, mister!" came a childish cry. "I ain't armed."

Paris and Cody exchanged a startled glance. Then together they leaned in to look through the doorway.

Chapter Thirteen

With a sense of relief, Cody flipped the light switch. Then he stepped farther into the shed, cautiously looking in the direction where Ma kept pinecones sealed in thirty-nine-gallon garbage bags. There, atop overstuffed plastic bags where he must have fallen, a boy defensively clutched a weathered backpack to his chest.

Cody's breath caught as he looked down into a mirror image of who he'd been as a five-year-old. The same shape of face, raven-dark hair and black-brown eyes filled with suspicion.

"Hey, there, young fella," Cody said softly, not wanting to further frighten the boy. "Who are you? And what are you doing here?"

For a long moment, their eyes locked and Cody got the distinct impression this kid had seen more than his share of the less-than-pleasant side of life, that he had every reason to be leery of Cody's sudden appearance in the doorway.

Oblivious of the pinecones being crushed under his weight, the boy clambered to his feet and slung his backpack over his shoulder. Then his chin jutted defiantly, his words tinged with a Texas accent. "I'm Deron Hawk. *D-E-R-O-N.* Who are *you* and what are *you* doing here?"

A Hawk.

Cody glanced to where Paris had joined him, reading immediately from her shocked expression that she'd seen the resemblance, too. The kid could be Cody's…

The boy stared unflinchingly from Cody to Paris and back again, but with a sinking feeling Cody recognized a too-familiar bravado that sent him hurtling back in time to his own childhood. He dismissed the boy's challenge for what it was. The kid was scared.

But from the looks of him, he was without a doubt a Hawk. Likely one of his brother's kids.

"I'm Cody. Cody *Hawk*. And this is Paris Perslow." He squatted to the same level as the boy and held out his hand for an introductory shake—which the glaring child didn't take him up on.

Cody glanced up at Paris, then back at the boy. "Well, Deron, can you tell us your dad's name?"

For a moment he thought the youngster wouldn't respond and he could almost sense Paris holding her breath. Did she really think the kid might be his? But apparently Deron was digesting Cody's words for, after a long pause, he thrust out an ice-cold hand for a man-to-man shake.

Where were the kid's gloves? His hat? The too-large jacket didn't look to be more than a layer of denim with a flannel lining and his sockless feet were thrust into well-worn tennis shoes.

"My dad is Carson Hawk and I'm here to see my granddad." The boy's eyes narrowed. "You don't look like a granddad."

Cody sensed Paris's smile.

"No, I'm not your granddad. I'm your dad's brother. Your uncle."

A flicker of uncertainty broke through the facade of the boy's bluster. "I'm supposed to stay with my granddad."

Stay? Did Ma know about this? In the midst of Dad's illness, had she forgotten to tell him of the anticipated arrival of her step-grandson, Cody's nephew?

Doubtful.

"Your grandfather...isn't here right now." No need to tell about the hospitalization. "Where's your dad?"

Deron shrugged, avoiding his gaze. "Dunno."

Cody didn't like the sound of that. "So he dumped you off here and—"

"Cody." Paris touched his shoulder and he looked up at her. "He's tired. He needs to get warm and something to eat."

He looked back at the boy. He did look tired. Cold. Hungry. "What did you have for breakfast?"

"Potato chips." He announced the fact as if proud of it.

"What about lunch?"

The boy lifted a shoulder as if the question was of no consequence. "Dad said granddad would feed me."

So he'd been dumped at the trailer since at least noon. Probably considerably longer.

Cody drew in a resigned breath. "What do you think about coming inside? Warming up? I imagine we can rustle up soup or a sandwich. You can eat while we let your grandfather—and your step-grandma—know you're here."

Alarm flashed through the boy's eyes as his glance darted toward the open door. For a moment, Cody feared the kid might take off. But the look disappeared as quickly as it had come and Cody rose slowly to his feet to place a reassuring hand on Deron's shoulder.

His brother's kid. Exactly what Ma didn't need right now.

"Paris?" His gaze met her troubled one. "Why don't you lead the way?"

Once inside the trailer, Paris settled Deron on the sofa, one of Ma's handmade afghans tucked in around him. Cody peeled out of his jacket, kicked up the heat a few notches, then headed to the adjoining kitchen to dig out a can of chicken noodle soup.

As he heated the soup, he could hear Paris's soothing words of reassurance. Promises that Deron was safe here. Praise for his bravery. Confirmation of his welcome.

Not too much later she joined him, her voice low. "He looks so much like you, Cody, I have to admit that for a moment I thought—"

"No worries," he likewise whispered. "There are no Cody Hawk juniors running around out there. And I guarantee you if there were, they wouldn't be abandoned on someone's doorstep."

They both glanced toward the living room where, warmed by the crocheted blanket, the exhausted boy now appeared to be dozing.

"So you think his parents abandoned him? That they didn't drop him off for a day or two?"

"You heard the kid. He said he's supposed to stay with his granddad. He doesn't know where his father is."

"But surely—"

Cody cut her off with a shake of his head. "I've never been interested in the lives of my half brothers, but I've picked up enough from Ma to know that Carson's left behind a string of women and offspring."

"But his mother...?"

"I'm sure we'll learn more soon enough."

Compassion filled her eyes. "It's so sad."

That was a nice way of putting it. If she'd ever doubted that Hawk men truly deserved their tarnished reputations, that they'd merely been victims of bad PR, Deron's unexpected arrival should still those doubts.

"Here," she said, gently pushing him aside and taking the spoon from his fingers. "Let me finish with this so you can call your mother."

"She should be on her way home by now. I won't call her while she's driving."

"Do you think she was expecting…company?"

He shook his head as he searched the cabinets for saltine crackers. "No, and she sure doesn't need this on top of everything else."

Paris's expression softened even further. "He was trying hard to be a tough little guy, wasn't he?"

Cody nodded. "You saw through it, too? He's scared to death."

"I can't imagine how parents could—"

"Hey!" a boyish voice demanded from the living room. "What's with the baby?"

Cody glanced to where Deron was now standing by the sofa, the afghan clutched around his slim shoulders.

"What baby is that, Deron?"

Poor kid. Regardless of whether or not Carson and the kid's mother had any intention of retrieving him, he'd see to it the boy had more appropriate winter wear. That was easy enough. But none of them were prepared to take on raising a kid.

Certainly not Ma, what with Dad's situation. What were they going to do with the little guy?

"What baby?" he asked again when Deron didn't respond.

The boy pointed to the ceramic nativity scene displayed on the coffee table. "*That* baby."

Cody caught Paris's look of alarm. The kid must be even more exhausted than they'd originally thought.

"That's baby Jesus," she reminded gently.

Deron's brow puckered. "Who is Jesus?"

Who is Jesus? Even the next day, Paris couldn't shake off Deron's question. To think that a boy his age, a kindergartner, hadn't any inkling of the birth of God's only son into the world seemed unimaginable. For a brief moment, she'd thought he might be teasing them, but one look in his dark, perplexed eyes quickly put an end to that assumption.

For Deron, Christmas was no more than Santa Claus and a red-nosed reindeer.

"You look pretty serious there." Cody glanced at her from where he'd laid down four ladder-back chairs in the bed of his truck. Paris had found them at the secondhand shop on Main Street that afternoon, intending them for a cozy holiday vignette at the clubhouse. Cody had been gracious enough to stop his work at Pine Shadow Ridge and meet her at the store to pick them up. "What are you thinking about?"

"Deron." She slipped her hands into her jacket pockets. "About how he didn't have a clue who Jesus is."

"I probably wasn't much more knowledgeable at that age than he is." Cody tossed a tarp across the chairs. "Ma didn't meet God herself until I was in high school. Even then, Dad wouldn't let me go to church with her—except, of course, the times when he thought we could get 'our fair share' from the congregation."

He shook his head.

"That's why you never went with your mother?"

"Right. The first time I probably heard the whole Christmas story—shepherds and angels and wise men and the works—was when I was a youngster and your mother read it to the neighborhood kids. I got included because Dad could hardly tell his employer's wife to take a hike."

"Really? That's the first time?"

"It was the first time it had ever been clear to me, not a jumbled kaleidoscope of disjointed stuff."

"Do you think I explained the true meaning of Christmas well enough to Deron?" She couldn't tell if any of it made sense to the boy. He listened, but didn't ask any questions, although he seemed fascinated by the nativity scene. Had she made the story sound as real as it truly was, not another fairy tale?

"You did an exceptional job," Cody said as he finished securing the tarp. "You kept it simple for a boy that age. Now we'll have to make sure we help him build on that foundation."

We.

Why did she like the sound of that? Cody probably meant it in a general sense, of course, not a personal one. Or maybe "we" meant him and his mother?

"My brother phoned the house late last night and talked to Ma." Cody adjusted the ball cap on his head. "Typical, though, that even when he heard about Dad's situation, he didn't offer a word of sympathy. He didn't care about the imposition on Dad's second wife at a time when she has her hands full. He's taking advantage, knowing Ma can't bear to turn Deron away."

"Did you talk to him, too?"

"No. But this morning he faxed documents to the school confirming that Ma and Dad will soon be Deron's legal guardians. It doesn't seem my softhearted mother has much of a choice."

"So he's going to stay? Poor little guy. Does he have siblings?"

"It sounds as if there are one or two older ones and a new baby. I guess a kid his age is too much to deal with for Carson's latest lady." He grimaced. "Ma's going to see the school guidance counselor to find out what's best—enrolling before Christmas break or after."

"Where is he today? Did your mother stay home with him?"

"No, he's with a next-door neighbor who has twin boys a year younger than him. Ma needed to talk to Dad without little ears listening in, and I can't drag him out to the maintenance building around heavy equipment and power tools."

"Maybe...I could help?" She couldn't bear to think of the child spending his day among strangers. Of course, she—like Lucy and Cody—was a stranger, too. But still...

He frowned. "What do you mean?"

"I'm pretty good with kids and I have several years of college toward an elementary education degree."

"Really? I didn't know that."

"Long story. I didn't finish. But children don't run in the other direction when they see me coming."

Cody folded his arms, the corners of his eyes crinkling. "Paris, there isn't a soul on the planet who would run when they saw you coming."

Warmth crept into her cheeks at Cody's candid compliment. "I could watch Deron once in a while. That way you wouldn't have to take off from the project and your mom could still spend time with your dad."

"Like you don't have enough to do?" He gazed thoughtfully at her for a moment, as if contemplating her suggestion, then shook his head. "Thanks for the offer, but we'll manage."

Disappointed, she watched as he started toward

the driver-side door, ready to head out to the clubhouse with the chairs.

"Cody?"

He paused, his hand on the door latch. "Yeah?"

She took a few steps toward him. "May I come
along?"

Uncertainty flickered in his eyes as he quickly
took in their Main Street surroundings. How many
times had she seen him do that, as if suspecting
they were being spied upon? Was he aware people
were talking about them, so he was trying to be
respectful of how his presence might incite gossip?

Heat crept into her cheeks as the moment drew
out. She shouldn't have asked to tag along. But after
yesterday, sharing in the discovery of Deron and
spending the evening making pinecone wreaths
with his mother, it seemed the wall between them
had crumbled slightly.

But apparently not enough.

Then his dark eyes swung back to her, and he
nodded.

"Sure. Come on."

Chapter Fourteen

Just a few nights ago, Paris's father had tracked him down and made veiled threats that should have sunk into Cody's brain. Yet today he found himself, bold as brass, driving down Main Street in his old loaner truck with the most beautiful woman in the world right beside him.

There is only so much I'll take of the games Hawks play. You got that?

Games Hawks play? What had he meant by that?

Cody cranked up the heat with an unsteady hand, but the shaky sensation didn't come from Merle Perslow's vague words of intimidation, but from the reality of Paris seated next to him.

He should have said no. It might have hurt her feelings, but she seemed oblivious to the fact that others had taken notice of the handful of moments they'd shared in recent weeks. People like his old classmate Jim Harper. Harry Campbell at the gatehouse. Paris's father.

Owen Fremont.

As they headed down the highway, he furtively glanced to where Paris gazed out the passenger-side window.

How many others had seen them together just now? He hated to think his presence, no matter how blameless, might blemish her standing in the community. She was young, innocent, and apparently didn't fully grasp the fact that a good reputation, once tarnished, couldn't easily be replaced, or she wouldn't have invited herself to ride along.

That's what Owen had tried, in his clumsy, selfish way, to get through to him and the point her father was undoubtedly trying to make. If he had to do it again, he wouldn't volunteer to fulfill Ma's contractual obligations. He'd pay the committee double—even triple—what his mother owed and wash his hands of it. But no, he'd let pride get in his way. Pride and the niggling hope that he might see Paris on occasion.

"Look, Cody!" She pointed up ahead, to the side of the tree-lined road. "Deer!"

He checked the rearview mirror for traffic, then slowed to pull off the road and cut the engine. A buck and two does lifted their heads, looking curiously in the direction of his truck.

"They're beautiful, aren't they?" she whispered.

"They aren't something I see on the streets of Phoenix, that's for sure."

In rapt silence they watched the wildlife move

slowly out of sight, then he started the truck and pulled onto the highway.

"You know, Cody, you've never told me what you've been doing the past twelve years. You mentioned Phoenix and your mother alluded to the fact that you have important things to attend to elsewhere. But that's all I know. It makes you somewhat a man of mystery."

Cody laughed. "I'd hardly call myself mysterious."

"What *have* you been doing with yourself?"

He'd already made clear he hadn't left a trail of women and kids behind him like Carson. But did she wonder if he'd gone from job to job, wandering aimlessly in this old relic of a pickup, one step ahead of the law?

He settled his ball cap more firmly on his head, keeping his eyes on the road. "A dozen years. That's a lot of territory to cover in a short jaunt to Pine Shadow Ridge."

"Try the CliffsNotes version."

So she really wanted to know? It wasn't every day that a woman like Paris asked to know more about him.

"Well, let's see…" His memory flew to the last time he'd seen her before leaving town, the night he'd shown up on her doorstep. No, he wouldn't start there. "Long story made short…I hitchhiked down to the Valley of the Sun. Then—"

"You *hitchhiked* to Phoenix? Cody, that was a dangerous thing to do."

He lifted a shoulder, dismissing her concern. "Not so dangerous when you're picked up by a talkative old rancher who is glad for the company and grateful for help unloading a cantankerous bull at an outlying ranch down there."

Paris shook her head disapprovingly, but he continued. "Turns out that ride was a godsend. The ranch was owned by a prosperous building contractor who happened to be desperate for workers who could handle a hammer."

"Then what?"

"That contractor's son, Trevor, and I hit it off and, before I knew it, the family basically took me in as a second son." He never would have foreseen that there were people in the world who would believe the best of him.

"I'm sure they saw what a hard worker you were."

His heart swelled. She recognized that? Had she seen that when he was growing up?

"Mostly I think they saw what a messed-up kid I was and how easy it would be for me to fall into the same destructive patterns as my half brothers. Trevor's folks were authentic Christians, not just a Sunday-morning variety, and recognized I needed tough love and a strong foundation to stand on."

"You were almost eighteen when you left here, weren't you? So, shortly after that you gave your life to God?"

Cody cut her a regretful look. "Nope. It would be another eight years before it finally sank in that the relationship the Cane family had with God was one He was offering me, too."

"That's a long time."

"I had a lot to be grateful for to Arden and Mona. And Trev, of course. But I had a rebellious heart, Paris. A heart that, despite Arden's loving example, had me convinced God fit the mold of Leroy Hawk. Unforgiving. Unpredictable. Untrustworthy. As we've touched on before, I couldn't make peace with the two extremes of fatherhood—what I'd lived versus what the Bible claimed."

He let his foot off the gas and slowed for the turn to the gated property. "Suffice it to say, our Heavenly Father eventually won me over. That was about three years ago."

A glance in Paris's direction caught her pensive expression as she stared out the window.

"So you do construction work?"

"I'd just finished my business degree when the building boom bottomed out, and Trev and I searched for other opportunities. Loans weren't easy to come by, but we did our research, picked out neighborhoods that had a good chance of revival and started flipping houses."

Paris turned to him. "So you're buying homes and fixing them up to sell for a profit?"

"And our risk is paying off. The housing market is stabilizing and prices are on the rise. We have a growing, competent team—made up of returning veterans and craftsmen who'd been hit hard by the economic downturn—so we're doing less of the labor ourselves and spending more time on the management end. In fact…" He and Trev hadn't shared this with many outside Trevor's immediate family, but with Paris's interested gaze now focused on him, he couldn't resist. "We have a major investor we're waiting to hear back from any day now. Trev and I'd like to branch out from the Valley and see where we could go with this statewide."

"Wow!"

She sounded as excited about it as he felt. Did she recognize that, while he might not yet be running in the same financial circles as her Owen Fremont, this poor kid from Canyon Springs had made good? "Yeah, we're pumped about it."

"I can see why. Do you think—" Her cell phone chimed, cutting her short. She pulled the phone from her pocket and glanced down at the caller ID, then back at him. "I'm sorry, Cody. I should take this."

A muscle tightened in his jaw.

Owen, no doubt.

Chapter Fifteen

"I took the liberty of picking up that velvet gown for you," Dalton's mother said, getting right to the purpose of her call. "I'll drop it off in the next day or two."

Paris self-consciously turned slightly away from Cody, but before she could respond, Elizabeth continued.

"By the way, I spoke with Parker's mother... and confirmed he'll be in town the weekend of the gala."

"Elizabeth, I thought I—"

"Now, now...I merely inquired about his plans while he's here and she's certain he wouldn't be opposed to acting as your escort."

"I already told you I don't need an escort," Paris stated, acutely aware of the man beside her. "I'm going to be far too busy for that."

"Nevertheless, consider the dress an early Christmas present. But don't wait too long to make up your mind about Parker. He's a nice young man with excellent prospects."

As soon as Elizabeth uttered a stiff goodbye, Paris shut off her phone. "You wouldn't happen to own a tux, would you, Cody? And be free the night of the Christmas gala?"

How did *that* pop out of her mouth?

He gave a halfhearted laugh as they headed toward the clubhouse nestled in the trees. "It sounds as if Mrs. Herrington has someone lined up for the occasion already."

Paris slipped the phone back into her pocket. "She won't let it go. She and Dad keep pushing Parker at me."

Cody's forehead creased. "Parker?"

"Parker Herrington. Dalton's cousin."

"But why would they… I thought… Aren't you seeing Owen Fremont?"

She almost choked. "Are you kidding me? No way."

"I have to admit I'm relieved to hear that."

He was? "Unfortunately, Elizabeth has already bought the dress."

He cast her a startled look. "A wedding dress?"

"No, silly." Paris made a face. "A gown for the Christmas gala. Are you sure you don't have a tux squirreled away someplace?"

How had she garnered the courage to even think such a thing, let alone boldly ask him? But it made sense. She was the head of this year's committee.

Cody was the decorative designer in his mother's stead. Who could possibly object?

"From the side of the conversation I heard," he said, injecting a teasing tone into his words, "it doesn't appear as if an escort will get any personal attention from the prettiest gal at the event. So, what, if you don't mind my asking, would be in it for me?"

Paris perked up. If Cody would come with her, that would relieve her from being saddled with Parker and would keep Owen at a distance, as well. "Great food. Live band. Hearing the oohs and aahs as everyone admires your artistic endeavors—how great you look in a tux."

Cody pulled the truck up beside the clubhouse and cut the engine. "You've never seen me in a tux."

She raised a brow. "I have a vivid imagination, Mr. Hawk."

A smile tugged at his lips and her heart rate sped up in an almost giddy rush of expectation.

"So," she challenged, looking him in the eye, "how about it?"

He'd give anything to waltz Paris around the dance floor in front of the astonished faces of the town's elite, but there was no way he'd indulge in a dream like that. Even if she was too naive, too idealistic, to recognize it, a move like that would be social suicide. He couldn't allow her to do that to herself.

Reluctantly he broke eye contact to open the driver-side door, buying himself a few moments to gather his thoughts as he made his way to let down the truck's tailgate. Paris joined him as he untied the tarp.

"It would be fun, Cody, wouldn't it? To see everyone enjoying your hard work? Your mother turned me down when I invited her but, if you were going, maybe she'd be willing to come, too."

No fair dragging Ma into this. But he still couldn't put Paris at risk. Couldn't risk, either, having Merle Perslow cut short the compensation he'd agreed to for Dad. In another few weeks, maybe a month, Cody might be in a more secure position financially to field that possibility, but in the meantime...

"I appreciate your invitation, Paris." He raised the tarp off the chairs. "But once I wrap up this project, I've got to head down the mountain and relieve my business partner. He's been carrying much of the load since I've been up here."

He lifted down a chair and glanced in her direction, regret stabbing at the disappointment reflected in her eyes. Was he nuts for finding excuses not to escort her to the charity event? But he didn't really have a choice. He cared too much for her.

"You couldn't stay in town a few extra nights?" The committee made arrangements for a breakdown crew. There would be no need for him to oversee that. Once he set everything up Thursday night, made sure everything was in working order, he could hand the reins to others.

He lifted down another chair, not meeting Paris's hopeful gaze. "Trevor's been a good sport about my absence, but he has little kids and with Christmas fast approaching…"

"Yeah, little kids and Christmas." She appeared to force a smile, as if at last giving up on her ill-thought-out campaign to get him to the gala. "I guess you'll have to contact Santa, won't you? Let him know where Deron is this year."

Cody almost dropped the third chair. "Santa?"

"You planned to buy him a gift anyway, didn't you?"

"I hadn't thought about anything beyond getting him warmer clothes." He should have taken care of that this morning before Ma sent the boy off for the day. The kid needed new socks, underwear and several changes of clothes in addition to winter outerwear. No way was he shipping his nephew off to his first day in Canyon Springs' kindergarten unless he was dressed as well as any kid in town.

"That jacket he had on didn't look suitable for a high-country winter," she agreed. "He didn't bring much in the way of personal items or toys with him, either. Did you notice? Only a pocketknife and a baseball."

"Yeah, and I took the knife away from him. He

was none too happy with me, but I didn't figure Ma's neighbor would want him showing it off to her twins or getting into any mischief with it."

"No, I imagine not."

Cody turned back to the truck and lifted out the final chair. "Where do you want these?"

"Just outside the cloak room, next to the oak side table. I can show you." Paris picked up one of the chairs and Cody hefted the other three. "I'll place a battery-operated lantern on the table and it will make a cozy area where people can sit to remove their boots should it decide to snow."

Once inside, Paris showed him where the chairs went. Then, before he knew it, he'd ushered her back into the truck and dropped her off at her SUV. If anyone had taken notice of Paris when she'd climbed into his truck, their brief journey and swift return couldn't ignite too much talk.

Could it?

"I don't like this color."

"You don't like blue?" Cody looked down at his nephew, who shrugged impatiently out of the navy insulated jacket they'd found at Dix's Woodland Warehouse Friday morning. What kid didn't like blue?

"Well, then, what color do you want?" For a kid who'd shown up on their doorstep with next to nothing, he sure was picky. They'd gone through this with the shirts, jeans, underwear and socks at the discount store, too. Cody didn't look forward to tackling boots today, but more snow was in the forecast.

The boy pointed to another jacket.

"That's blue, Deron."

"Uh-uh. Not the same kind."

No, royal wasn't the same as navy. Apparently the kid knew his crayon colors.

Cody knelt to help Deron into the jacket, zipped it and then turned him from side to side to make sure it fit well.

"So, does this one work for you?"

Deron nodded, a grin widening as he lifted his hand for a high five, and Cody's heart did a three-sixty in his chest. This little guy's parents had dumped him on strangers and he could smile like that?

Deron had been slow to warm up to Cody. He'd kept his distance, which led Cody to believe Carson had more in common with Leroy Hawk than he'd hoped. Anger sired anger. Abuse, abuse. But he hoped that smile would be the first of many.

The bells above the door announced yet another shopper as Cody hustled to get Deron to pick out his final items. Their shopping excursion was taking way too much time, but the boy wasn't inclined to be rushed. Cody thrust a pair of brown gloves at him, but the boy immediately pushed away his offering.

Here we go again.

"I like that coat, Deron," a familiar female voice chimed in.

Cody glanced at Paris, noticing with pleasure that her cheeks were rosy from the cold, a red scarf snuggled at the neck of her teddy-bear coat. He'd tossed and turned last night, thinking about her invitation to the gala. But he kept coming back to the same conclusion. He couldn't escort her.

But would that force her to invite the Parker guy?

Paris reached for a red knit cap, then knelt down by Deron. "Ooh, I like this one."

"He doesn't like navy blue," Cody supplied, pleased he could share that insight.

She gave him a perplexed look. "This isn't navy blue, is it?"

"No, no, I meant…" His words faded as their gazes held. Suddenly he had no idea what he'd meant or what he was doing in Dix's looking at kid gear.

"Paris." Deron patted her arm to get her attention. "Uncle Cody says I can have gloves *and* mittens."

She focused again on the boy. "He does, does he? Maybe you can get red ones to match this hat."

"Okay." Deron turned back to the rack without argument.

What was the deal with that? Cody had battled him every step of the way that morning. Did his nephew think the pretty Miss Perslow was a more reliable source of fashion advice?

"These!" Deron triumphantly held up a pair of red fleece-lined mittens in one hand and insulated red gloves in the other.

Cody grabbed a red wool scarf from the rack and handed it to Deron, but the boy turned to Paris, his eyes questioning. She nodded and the kid looped it happily around his neck.

Go figure.

At least now he had some ideas of what to get his nephew for Christmas. Not that the kid asked for anything. He'd actually been unusually quiet, his eyes rounding at the floor-to-ceiling kid stuff at the discount store. It now seemed wise, however, to run his ideas by Paris if he didn't want to wind up with one disappointed kid on Christmas day.

"Well, let's get going, bud." He placed his hand on Deron's shoulder as Paris rose to her feet.

"Now we're going to get boots," the boy informed her, lifting hopeful eyes to hers. "You can come, too."

Chapter Sixteen

Paris glanced uncertainly at Cody, who looked slightly startled at his nephew's announcement, then back at Deron. "Thank you for inviting me, but—"

"Paris?" Cody raised his brows in appeal. "Believe me, the whole ordeal will go faster if you come."

She laughed. Poor guy. "Okay. Let me pick up a few things here and we can be on our way."

They paid for their purchases, then out on the street Deron reached for her hand. Her heart melted at the unexpected gesture of acceptance. Did he miss his mother? Did he wonder why he'd been thrust into a world of strangers?

But she was even less prepared when he grabbed hold of Cody's hand with his free one, and suddenly the three of them were linked as a unit. As a family.

Cody glanced at her and she could tell that he, too, was touched by the child's openness but discomfited by the happy domestic scenario. Nevertheless, they moved past the shops, hands still held.

"You two have such a cute boy," a teenage girl gushed as she and a friend paused outside a store.

Cody's eyes met Paris's as a wave of mortification mixed with pleasure washed through her. It was an easy enough mistake to think Cody's nephew was his son, of course, but fortunately, Deron appeared oblivious of the comment as he skipped along between them as if he hadn't a care in the world. Kids were amazing. So resilient.

Inside one of Canyon Springs' outdoor gear shops, she and Cody consulted comfortably, almost as if shopping together for a small boy were an everyday occurrence. Paris couldn't help but enjoy these fleeting shared moments. Cody was a good and generous man, ensuring that a nephew he'd never laid eyes on until a few days ago was well outfitted.

Watching uncle and nephew together, she couldn't help but remember how very little Cody had materially as a kid, yet how proudly he'd held up his head in spite of cruel jeers. Clearly, if he had anything to say about it, Deron's experiences in Canyon Springs wouldn't be anything like his uncle's.

They quickly found Deron a pair of quality snow boots. Waterproof and lined for warmth, they were perfect for tackling snowdrifts and slushy puddles the boy would no doubt find his way into.

"See? That wasn't so bad," she whispered to Cody at the checkout counter.

A corner of his mouth turned up. "You got off lucky, woman."

She yelped a soft laugh and the young male clerk looked up at her with a smile. She smiled back. In fact, she still felt like smiling at everyone she saw as they exited the store. It had been a long time since she'd felt like this.

Unburdened. Free. Happy.

She glanced at Cody who was exchanging teasing remarks with his nephew, the fact that it was in his presence that she was feeling this way not lost on her. There was something about him…so competent, responsible, caring. With him she felt a sense of security that she'd not felt with any other man.

As good of a person as Dalton had been, as much as she'd cared for him as a dear friend, she hadn't experienced that sense of peace and belonging that she increasingly felt when in the company of Cody Hawk.

Which was crazy. He would be in town only a short while longer. Obviously he didn't share her budding feelings or he'd have accepted her invitation to the gala. Or did he not recognize she was opening the door, even if only a crack, for him to step through if he wanted to?

"How about a cup of hot chocolate, Paris?" Cody

studied her, as if wondering at her lengthy stretch of silence. "Deron says he's game."

"Me, too." But she didn't feel as over-the-top giddy as she had a few moments ago.

Even if Cody did share her feelings, what kind of future could they hope to have together? Dad would never welcome a son of Leroy Hawk. Nor would the brokenhearted Elizabeth receive him with open arms. How could Paris live with letting down those who loved her?

"You okay?" Cody cocked his head as he held open the door to Camilla's Café, the scent of fresh-baked bread and cookies wafting onto the street.

"I'm fine." Pushing back her coat cuff to look at her wristwatch she gasped, then stepped away from the door. "I can't believe it. It's almost eleven-thirty."

"So? Have soup and a sandwich instead. My treat."

"I have to meet Macy and Jake at Kit's Lodge. We're having lunch, then meeting with the caterer to go over details for their Saturday wedding. Tonight's the rehearsal dinner, too." She lifted the shopping bag. "I'd gone out to pick up a few things when I ran into you and Deron. I need to drop these off at the office before my appointment and make certain nothing pressing has come up in my absence."

Was that disappointment in Cody's eyes? It certainly was in Deron's. But her own feelings were mixed. As delightful as time spent with these two handsome males might be, she had to get her head back in the real world.

"You hafta come." Deron's forehead creased as he tugged on her sleeve, his eyes troubled.

"I wish I could, but you'll still have fun. Camilla's makes the best hot chocolate in the whole wide world." She sneaked a glance at Cody. "Make sure your uncle gets you whipped cream on top. With cinnamon."

"Doesn't that sound good, Deron?" Cody placed a consoling hand on the boy's shoulder when he didn't respond. "Thanks again, Paris, for playing shopping assistant."

"You're welcome."

"I may call on you again to talk *C-H-R-I...*" Nodding toward Deron who was still frowning up at Paris, he let his words drift off. Then he turned his nephew toward the open café door. "Come on, kid, let's see what this place has to offer."

Disappointed at missing out, even though it had been her own decision, Paris didn't linger outside but hurried back to the office.

Please, Lord, help me to stop thinking about Cody Hawk.

"Paris is your girlfriend, huh?" Deron licked the last of the whipped cream from the rim of the hot chocolate mug, his watchful eyes on Cody.

Where'd his nephew get an idea like that? He

glanced around, hoping no one had overheard. Paris didn't need to be the focus of gossip and he sure didn't want Deron's vocal assumption getting back to her father via the Canyon Springs grapevine. He lowered his voice. "No, she's not my girlfriend."

"How come?" his nephew pushed aside the mug and reached for a remaining French fry that had accompanied his half sandwich. "You can have more than one girlfriend. My dad does."

Cody held back a look of disgust at Deron's matter-of-fact assessment. His half brother's lifestyle wasn't one to which a little boy should have had to be exposed. That was one point in Leroy Hawk's favor. To Cody's knowledge, Dad never stepped out on Ma, and he'd even managed to settle himself down once they'd come to Canyon Springs.

"Paris is a friend. All girls who are friends don't have to be girlfriends."

"Oh." Deron swirled the French fry through a mound of ketchup, then looked up at Cody with one eye squinted. "But she'd be a good girlfriend, huh?"

She'd not only make a good girlfriend, but a good wife. A good mother. Cody shook his head as he folded his napkin and placed it on the table, dismayed at how easily those conclusions had slipped into his mind.

"Yeah, Deron, she would make a good girlfriend."

The boy smiled as though satisfied with his

uncle's response. But as Cody knew too well, hoping, wishing and praying didn't always make dreams come true.

It was all she could do not to collapse at the conclusion of Macy and Jake's wedding reception Saturday afternoon. One wedding down. Two to go.

Thankfully, she wasn't responsible for cleanup and didn't intend to pitch in, as she often did at weddings in the past. She was tired.

And a little melancholy.

It had been a lovely ceremony and celebration afterward, the Christmas colors a beautiful contrast to the bride's vintage dress and the snow-white tiered cake with its holly accents. The bride's mother had even shown up after all. But, throughout, Paris's thoughts drifted to Cody. To Dalton. Back to Cody.

So what should she do now? Crashing at home held vast appeal but, with a few hours of daylight remaining, she returned there only briefly to change clothes before making her way to Pine Shadow Ridge. Last week Cody had set up worktables for her in the clubhouse ballroom, but had he settled her there on a pretense of it being more comfy than the maintenance building when he really wanted to keep her at a distance?

It was dark by the time she secured a final pine-cone with a generous dab of hot glue, then stepped back with a sense of satisfaction to view another completed wreath. Cody might not want her hanging around, but she knew he appreciated her assistance with the smaller decorative items while he focused on the larger ones.

Somewhere in the building she heard the echoing sound of a door closing and heavy footsteps on the tiled hallway floor. She turned, her heart beating faster in foolish anticipation as Cody stepped through the door.

His dark eyes lighted on her. "How'd the wedding go?"

"Beautiful. I imagine Macy's blog will feature a few photos this week. You should check it out."

"I may do that." He moved to the worktables to study the growing stock of wreaths, the fresh scent of the outdoors clinging to him. "How long have you been here?"

She turned back to the table and picked up the glue gun, determined to start another wreath tonight. "About three hours."

Cody leaned down to unplug the glue gun. "Then it's time to call it quits."

"If I want to get these done," she said, plugging the device back in, "I have to squeeze in the time when I can."

"*Have* to? Volunteers come in this week for the final push. It will get done. Do you mind my asking why you're packing your days with nonstop activity? Sharon says you got roped into the weddings at the last minute. Why didn't you say no?"

She shrugged. "I guess I want everything to be perfect for the brides and grooms on their special day."

And to somehow drive away the dark cloud of guilt that had hung over her for three and a half years.

"Perfect?" The corners of Cody's mouth turned downward. "That's a high bar you've set for yourself, don't you think? You're going to burn out before Christmas even gets here. You should take a day off to rest."

"Maybe *after* Christmas." She looked around at the spacious, raftered room, picturing all that remained to be done. "The trees arrive on Monday. Do you think they'll decorate themselves? That the faux gift packages to go under them will pop into their paper and bows on their own?"

"No. But where's the time for peace on earth?"

"I don't have—"

"No excuses." He took the glue gun from her hand, uplugged it once again, then placed it in its stand. Striding to where she'd tossed her coat and scarf over the back of a chair, he looped the scarf around his neck. Then picking up her coat, he turned to hold it open so she'd only have to step up and slip her arms into the sleeves. "Come on, Paris. It's a beautiful night out there. I have something I want to show you."

Chapter Seventeen

Despite his assurances that they were on-target to meet the deadline, Cody couldn't afford to lose an evening of work. He'd driven over to see Dad that afternoon—another awkward visit—and had just returned to town. But Paris was wearing herself out and something was clearly troubling her. As tragically as her wedding plans had ended, how could the trio of beaming brides and grooms *not* get to her?

He lifted the open coat invitingly, an idea having surfaced that would get her mind off whatever was weighing her down. "So what are we waiting for, hmm?"

She hesitated, indecision flickering in her eyes, then at last a weary smile curved. "Okay. You win."

He helped her into her coat, then they took a few minutes to straighten things up before stepping outside into the crisp night air. He cupped her elbow, guiding her toward his truck.

"Where are we going?"

"Wait and see."

Once they settled into the still-toasty-warm vehicle, he started the engine and flipped on the headlights. With the dashboard faintly illuminating the interior, he drove out of the parking lot and down one of the residential property's streets.

"I got good news today." It was hard to keep the elation out of his voice.

"What would that be?"

"My business partner received a call from that potential investor I told you about." He glanced in her direction. "It's a go."

"Cody!" Her eyes lit up as she squeezed his arm. "That's not good news, that's *wonderful* news. I'm so happy for you."

"We're pretty pleased to have reached this milestone." Trevor had been flying so high when he'd called that Cody could hardly pry the details out of him. "It's not without risk, but it's a promising start."

"Very promising, I'd say. From what you've told me, you and your partner have put a tremendous amount of time, muscle and brainpower into your business. Maybe now you can reap the rewards."

"That's what we're hoping." It would certainly put him and Trevor on more solid ground financially, which would no doubt delight Trev's wife. It would bolster Cody's ability to care for his folks, as well. Maybe to buy a home, settle down…

He slowed for a turn down a winding side street, headlights piercing the darkness. Not a single house showed signs of life. "It's really quiet around here in the winter, isn't it?"

"It is. But it's nice, too. While I enjoy the tourist activity during the summer, there's something special about Canyon Springs when we're basically back to the locals."

"I'd forgotten what a contrast the seasons could be here, not only weatherwise, but the vibe, as well."

Ah, there it was—the cul-de-sac he was looking for. With the thick stand of trees now blocking streetlights, he drove through the undeveloped area, then pulled the truck to a stop in the middle of a circular pavement that marked the end of the street. Cut the engine.

Paris poked him playfully in the arm. "This is what you wanted me to see, Cody? A dead end?"

"Oh, ye of little faith." He stepped out. "Stay right where you are."

He snagged three heavy Mexican blankets he kept stashed behind the seat and draped them over his arm. Then, having shut the door, he loped around to the passenger side to help Paris from the truck.

"What are you up to?" He could hear the curiosity in her teasing tone.

"Hang on." Leading her to the front side of the

truck, he then wrapped one of the big blankets around her shoulders.

She gave a startled gasp as he lifted her up to sit on the truck's hood and motioned for her to scoot back and lean against the windshield where he tucked another blanket behind her.

"Oooh. The truck hood is cozy warm."

"I figured it would be. I just got back from Show Low." He moved to the opposite side and pulled himself up on the hood to settle in beside her, then spread the last blanket across their legs.

"Tell me again what we're doing here?" She sounded nervous now.

"I find the dark is usually the best place for star-gazing." He leaned back against the windshield and pointed skyward. "Agree?"

Together they lifted their eyes to the heavens.

"Oh, my," Paris whispered.

At the more-than-mile-high elevation, devoid of artificial lights, starlight popped out against the inky blackness overhead in breathtaking clarity. Hundreds of them. Thousands. Millions. Sweeping across the universe in a display that put man-made holiday lights to humble shame.

"'Lift up your eyes and look to the heavens,'" Cody softly quoted the verse from the Book of Isaiah. "'Who created all these? He who brings out the starry host one by one and calls forth each of them by name.'"

"Can you imagine?" Paris kept her voice low,

clearly as awed as he was by the magnificence above. "Not only having the imagination and power to create the stars, but to name every single one?"

"Amazing, isn't it?" He made a sweeping motion to the starry host above. "The Good Book says God has clearly made Himself known to mankind, His eternal power and divine nature, through His creation."

A ripple of awareness of that truth coursed through Cody as he stared into the night. But he was also acutely aware of Paris, the brush of her coat sleeve against his, the ever-so-faint scent of her perfume. For quite some time they gazed in rapt silence at the display above.

"Cody?" Paris finally broke the stillness.

"Yeah?"

"Did you miss Canyon Springs?"

"I can't say I did. I missed Ma, of course, and…" He glanced at her, softly illuminated in the dim light. "And another special person."

She looked away, sensing the significance of what he'd said. *Good going, Hawk. Back off.* She might not be seeing Owen and was being pressured to get involved with Parker, but that didn't mean she'd want *him* in her life. Besides, as her father had often reminded him…*you have no business looking on the high shelf.*

He cleared his throat. "I kept in touch with Ma, but basically cut myself off from the past."

Or he'd tried to, anyway.

"I rarely looked at the online paper for local news," he continued. "And I forbade Ma to fill in the blanks. I didn't want to be kept apprised of the comings and goings of folks in Canyon Springs. That's why...why I didn't know about Dalton's passing."

He heard her soft intake of breath at the mention of her fiancé's name.

"I know it's been rough," he continued gently. "It's taken courage to go on without someone you love, to commit to helping those brides after your own loss."

"Please, Cody, not you, too." She abruptly drew the blanket more closely around her shoulders and shifted away from him to again stare into the night.

He should have kept his mouth shut about the weddings. About Dalton. "I didn't mean to upset you. I'm sorry, Paris."

She shook her head. "No, don't apologize. It's just that..."

"Just what?"

She sighed, but didn't look at him. "Everyone treats me with kid gloves, as Dalton's grieving widow. Elizabeth. Dad. The entire town. Everyone pitying me. Now *you*."

He studied her a long moment, weighing his words. "I feel badly about your losing Dalton. But I can't say that I *pity* you. Not if you mean that I think of you in a negative sense, think lesser of you because of your situation."

Like someone might pity a kid growing up on the wrong side of the tracks?

She turned to him. "My situation? You have no idea what my situation is. Nobody does."

As he'd suspected, unresolved grief. The weddings had resurrected it in a way she hadn't been prepared for. "Why don't you tell me, then? I'm a good listener."

For several long moments he didn't think she would respond. Then came a soft sigh.

"Nobody understands, Cody, because…" He felt her gaze piercing into his, sensed the struggle she was having to get the words out. "Nobody knows I'm responsible for Dalton's death."

His heart jolted. "Say again?"

"You heard me." Her voice quavered. "If it weren't for me, Dalton would be alive today."

Her words made no sense. He'd gone back and read the coverage of that tragedy. Every detail. Nothing indicated she was at fault. "He died in a car accident, Paris. Hit by a drunk driver. You weren't even with him."

"No…but he came home days earlier than planned because *I* asked him to. Don't you see, Cody? He came home early and was hit head-on by that drunk."

Cody groaned as he slid his arm around her, pulling her close. She didn't resist, but slipped her hands free of her blanket to cling to the front of his jacket.

"It wasn't your fault, Paris. It's not."

"It is. I asked him to come home early because…" She drew a ragged breath. "I wanted to break up with him."

She intended to break up with Dalton? Why?

"I woke up one morning a few weeks before my wedding day, looked around at happily married couples and realized something was missing in our relationship. Suddenly I recognized we weren't well-matched despite our similar backgrounds and the fact that our parents were so excited about joining our two families."

"Had you been pressured, like you're now feeling with Parker?"

She shook her head. "I wouldn't call it pressured. It was more like encouraged. Expected. I'd gone along willingly, eager to please. It wasn't as if Dalton and I didn't like each other. Everyone in town thought we'd make a perfect couple."

"But not you?"

"I did at first." She gave a little sigh. "It's hard to explain, but our getting together was assumed. Like a son and daughter who unquestioningly join the family firm. I threw myself into wedding preparations, attempting, I know now, to shut out that still, small voice trying to get my attention."

"I can relate to that." How many years had he allowed his relationship with Dad to figuratively press hands against his own ears to block out God's persistent call?

"Suddenly my eyes were opened that when we talked on the phone, we never talked about anything that mattered to either of us. Only about the wedding plans. That's when I realized I wasn't what he needed in a wife."

"Nor was he what you needed in a husband," Cody said quietly. "Don't forget, Paris, your needs are equally important."

"I'm coming to recognize that now, to ask myself what kind of marriage is it if you can't share from the heart. From the soul? You know, if you don't know each other well enough to trust each other with that part of yourself? But after our engagement announcement, I'd focused on planning that one stupid day out of my entire life. I tried to please everyone around me, rather than listening to what God was trying to tell me."

"What did Dalton have to say about it?"

He felt her shrug. "I got a sense that he might have misgivings as well, but I didn't have the opportunity to tell him what I've told you. I wanted to do that in person, face-to-face. So I'll never know for sure."

"Men aren't dimwits. I imagine he sensed you didn't feel the way a bride should feel and welcomed your request to come home early. He may have wanted out, too, but—like you—he knew there would be repercussions in the family and he didn't want to hurt you."

She burrowed closer to Cody as if to absorb his

reassurance. He gently stroked the length of her silky hair as she pressed against him. So warm. Fragile.

"You're not responsible for Dalton's death, Paris. He chose to come home when he did, just like someone wrongly chose to drive drunk that night. You need to forgive yourself."

Was she listening to what he was saying? Really listening and allowing God to heal her broken, fearful heart?

Paris slowly lifted her gaze to the starry expanse that clearly spoke God's presence and His love to those who chose to hear. He sensed her relax against him, to accept a peace long absent, held at arm's length by her refusal to receive it.

Thank You, Lord. Thank You.

Cody's drew her closer, his head now resting gently against her hair.

"It's not that I didn't care for Dalton," she whispered into the night. "I did. But not…not the way I'm coming to care for you."

There. She'd said it.

Cody's arms tightened around her, but he didn't respond.

What must he think of her? She'd admitted to being responsible for her fiancé's death, then almost in the next breath confessed to having feelings for Cody. A depth of feelings that Dalton had never inspired. But her statement was true. There was a peace here in Cody's arms that she'd never found in Dalton's, a sense of God smiling down on her. On them.

She drew back to look at him. His eyes were closed, almost as if in prayer. Was he asking God how to respond to her shocking confession?

"Cody?" she said softly, her fingers tightening on the front of his jacket, brushing the soft wool of the scarf he'd earlier flung around his neck. Her scarf.

He opened his eyes and her breath caught. Compassion filled his gaze...and something else. He'd always looked at her in a way other boys—and later men—never had. But his eyes now met hers with a vulnerable, questioning intent, as if he wasn't sure he'd correctly understood what she'd told him.

She nodded slightly, a tiny smile encouraging.

"Paris?" he said softly, his gaze flickering from her eyes to her mouth and back to her eyes. And yet he still hesitated.

She grasped the edges of the scarf looped around his neck and tugged him gently toward her, a teasing lilt in her tone. "What are you waiting for, Mr. Hawk?"

His dark eyes sparked at her challenge, a corner of his mouth turning up. Then he once again closed his eyes and leaned in to touch his lips to hers.

Chapter Eighteen

No business. No business. No business.

His heart almost exploding from his chest and Merle's derisive words hammering through his brain, Cody nevertheless enveloped Paris in his arms, his mouth joining hers in a tender dance of love.

How long he'd dreamed of this moment. Dreamed of her soft lips pressed against his as her hands wound around his neck to draw him even closer. Or maybe he *was* dreaming. Right now. This very minute. But if he took it slow, savored every precious second, could he keep himself from waking? Could he stay right here with her in his arms forever?

Too soon she pulled back slightly and he cupped her face in his hands, loath to let her go, as his thumb caressed the scar he knew to be on her lower lip. At the quick intake of her breath, he leaned in again to touch his lips to that corner of her mouth, then drew back.

"Do you remember the day we first met, Paris? On the playground?"

Still breathless, she nodded.

"You were the sweetest, most beautiful girl I'd ever known."

"And you were my hero come to life."

He swallowed, not daring to believe that startling revelation. "I was?"

She nodded again. "From the very beginning."

"I...I never knew that."

"You were. You *are*."

He *had* to be dreaming. This was Paris Perslow snuggled in his arms, confessing secrets of the heart he'd never imagined hearing. He closed his eyes and touched his lips to her forehead, willing himself not to wake.

Please, not yet. Not yet.

"Do you remember," she said softly, "the night you came to see me before you left town?"

"Yeah. That's the night you sent me packing."

"I didn't want to. You said you loved me, remember? And I so badly wanted you to kiss me."

"Then why...?" He'd laid his heart at her feet that night. Ripped it right out and dared offer it, only to have her push him away. She'd loved him twelve years ago?

"Because..." She ducked her head, almost as if in shame. "I knew my Dad would never..."

Cody's spirits deflated. "Because I was the son of Leroy Hawk."

She nodded and, heart heavy, Cody pulled away to slide off the driver's side of the hood. Then he walked to the other side to help her down, as well. It was colder now. He needed to let her get home and then he needed to get back to work.

Tucking the blanket more securely around her, he gently tilted her chin to look up at him. "I'm still the son of Leroy Hawk, Paris."

"I know."

"Nothing's changed."

"But it has," she said, reaching for his hand as if sensing his heart pulling away. "*We* have."

"Have we? You're still the beautiful belle of Canyon Springs. I'm still a no-good Hawk."

Her grip tightened. "You're a Hawk who now walks with God. A man who's proven himself to be a trustworthy man of integrity, a savvy business professional, a kindhearted man who looks after his mother and now a nephew."

His heart swelled at her words of praise. She saw that in him? "But what about you, Paris? You say I've changed. But have you?"

She'd turned him away once. Cracked open his heart. While she'd returned his kisses tonight, did she have it in her to stand up to her father? And even if she could, did he have it in him to ask her to?

"I'm no longer a sixteen-year-old, Cody." She

pulled her hands free to cross her arms, her chin lifting as if daring him to contradict her. "I'm a woman who is coming to realize I've spent too much of my life attempting to please people because I was afraid if I said no, they wouldn't love me. I've allowed others to dictate how *they* think God wants me to live my life rather than allowing Him to get close enough to me so that I know and trust His voice. Is that enough change for you?"

"Paris—"

"Once, a long time ago," she cut in, looking him in the eye, "you told me you loved me. Do you… still?"

The love he'd confessed twelve years ago was only a shadow of what he understood love to be now. While an important part of it, love was more than ramped-up hormones and wild crazy feelings. So much more.

"I do, Paris. I've always loved you."

She blinked rapidly, then drew a shaky breath. "I love you, too."

He opened his arms and without hesitation, Paris stepped into them, slipped her arms around his waist and laid her head against his chest.

"What do we do now, Cody?"

"What would you like to do?"

"I think…I'd like to spend the rest of my life with you."

He gazed skyward, searching for answers. For

wisdom. Here in this moment, alone together, all things seemed possible. All mountains could be climbed, all challenges overcome.

But he knew that wasn't real life. He was still a Hawk. Her father had harbored animosity toward him for as long as Cody could remember. Townspeople would be shocked that Paris would replace their beloved Dalton with a kid from the wrong side of town. A kid whose despised father drank too much, and whose half brothers left disreputable reputations in their wake.

"We should take it slow," he said at last, hating the thought of it. He'd marry her tonight if he had the power to snap his fingers and make everything right in their world.

"Because you don't believe I've changed, do you?" she said softly.

He looked down at her. "Of course I do."

"No. Right now you're thinking that at the first sign of disapproval I'll turn my back on you."

"I wouldn't blame you if you did. It's not going to be easy, Paris."

She tightened her arms around him. "The best things in life aren't always easy."

"No."

"But you don't trust me, do you? You don't believe when I say I love you, that I love you the way you say you love me." A determined gleam flashed in her eyes. "Come to the Christmas gala with me next week. Be my escort."

He stiffened. That was too public a venue for their first appearance as a couple. "Paris, I don't think—"

"Who's the scaredy-cat now?" She raised a delicate brow.

He frowned.

She laughed softly. "Ruffled your fur, did I? Come on. I think you'll discover your perceptions of this town are highly distorted."

Dare he tell her of the suspicious looks he'd encountered in recent weeks? How many times her father had warned him away?

"Paris—"

"You say you love me. Come. Please, Cody? For me?"

"*Something* is going on." Delaney's dancing eyes narrowed as she caught up with Paris in the parking lot after church Sunday morning. "I demand to know what it is."

"What are you talking about?"

"All during the service you had this secret smile thing going on." Delaney did her best to imitate it.

Paris laughed, her face warming under her friend's intense scrutiny. "It's Christmas. I'm happy."

"I'm not buying it. It's that Hawk guy, isn't it? Come on, fess up."

Paris glanced around to make sure no others exiting the church were within earshot, then took a deep breath. "He's going to be my escort for the Christmas gala."

Delaney gave a little yelp. "Get out of here. Are you kidding me?"

Paris shook her head, joy bubbling. It was fun to share happy news for a change. To remember how it had felt to be held by Cody. Kissed by him. She'd never felt like this before. Ever.

"Wow, Paris. I'm jealous." Delaney leaned in close, lowering her voice even further. "I absolutely cannot wait to see him in a tux."

"I'm looking forward to that, too." To her surprise, he said he owned one—that he'd attended a number of business and social functions in recent years with his business partner and his partner's parents that called for one. How many more things there must be that she didn't know about the grown-up Cody—or that he didn't know about her. He was right. They needed time to get to know each other.

But, hopefully, not *too* much time.

Delaney's smile widened. "I saw his mother in church this morning, but not him. Has he gone to the Valley to pick out a ring? Hmm?"

The prospect of an engagement, while enticing to think about, was premature. "Actually, his dad isn't doing well so he's in Show Low this morning.

I guess Leroy's kidneys are in worse shape than originally thought."

Delaney's smile faded. "From a lifetime of over-drinking."

"Probably."

"That's rough." Her friend gave Paris's arm a quick squeeze. "Look, I have to run, but we've got to get together. Soon. I want to hear all about Cody Hawk."

When Delaney departed, Paris drove home and fixed herself a light lunch—Dad was at his folks' house but Cody had promised to call her when he got back to Canyon Springs. She'd finished straightening the kitchen when the call came shortly before noon.

"How's your father?"

"Not doing so great. One of his kidneys is pretty well shot. The other isn't far behind. His doctors are considering removing the worst one, but they're hesitant with him still having ministrokes."

"I'm sorry, Cody."

"Yeah. Bad situation."

"How's your mother?"

"Hanging in there. She stayed home and took Deron to church this morning, but she just left to go see Dad. I don't like getting such a late start, but I'm taking the little guy with me to the Valley to get my tux. It will be a down-and-up trip and dark before we get back, but I thought you might like to go."

A long excursion with Cody? A chance to see his place? "I'd love to."

"Would you mind if we took your SUV? Deron's small for his age so I bought a car seat for him and it doesn't fit that well in my old truck."

"That's fine."

"You're home right now? By yourself?"

She knew he wanted to know if Dad was there before he showed up on her doorstep. "Just me. But why don't I come get you guys?"

That way Cody's vehicle wouldn't be sitting in the driveway at her place all afternoon. She scribbled a note to let Dad know she'd be out and taped it to the door leading from the garage to the utility room. He'd be certain to see it there if he returned before she did. Then she was off to pick up Cody and Deron and within thirty minutes they were heading down the mountain, Cody in the driver's seat.

"This is a sweet set of wheels," he commented a considerable distance from town, finally getting a word in edgewise. Deron, unlike his somewhat reticent uncle, revealed a gift of gab once he felt comfortable with those around him. From the moment Deron was fastened into the car seat behind them, the questions had been nonstop. Where had Paris been? Where were they going? What was a tux? Why were the trees so tall here? Was it going to snow again?

She'd fielded them all, enjoying the boy's chatter.

How could his parents give him up like that? Did they intend to come back for him? Ever?

Farther on, once they'd dropped off the Mogollon Rim, the ponderosas were a thing of the past. The rugged terrain's vegetation changed rapidly from the scrub oak and fragrant pinyon pine to ocotillo, prickly pear and majestic saguaro cactus. Deron's questions multiplied. Was Cody enjoying seeing their world through the eyes of a child as much as she was?

They reached Cody's home by three-thirty, an apartment in a shady, well-cared-for complex where she stepped out of the SUV to the delightful sound of birdsong, then assisted Cody in releasing Deron from his car seat.

"This is beautiful." She opened her arms wide, drinking in the sunshine and almost-seventy-degree temperature.

"Do you have a dog, Uncle Cody?" Deron asked, pushing eagerly past them as they entered the second-floor apartment.

"No, no dogs. Maybe someday when I get a place with a big yard or acreage."

Deron went off to explore and Paris found herself examining Cody's quarters with as much interest as the little boy. Flavored with a bold but tasteful color palette and Southwestern accents, the furniture was simple, the space uncluttered. Masculine. Like Cody.

"This is nice," she said, stepping through the

French doors and onto the balcony as Cody returned with his bagged tux, shirt, tie and shoes. He placed them on the back of the sofa, then joined her, motioning for them to sit at the patio table.

"I'm not here a whole lot, but it's home." His warm gaze lingered on her. "For now."

Suddenly shy, she glanced through the open door behind them. "Where'd Deron get off to?"

"He found my video games. He can't hurt them and they can't hurt him. All G-rated."

Cody having correctly read the concern in her question, she relaxed in the padded chair. "I can't believe the contrast in the weather between here and a few hours north. While the summertime heat isn't anything I'd care to deal with, *this* I could handle."

"You'd consider leaving Canyon Springs?"

That would be an issue, wouldn't it? Where to live, assuming Cody's suggestion to "take it slow" ended where she hoped and prayed it would.

"I already decided to leave." At his raised brow, she quickly amended, "Even before you came back, before…us…I knew I needed to start somewhere fresh."

"Where do you plan to go?"

Did he think her future might be in opposition to his? That she'd be dashing off to adventures in New York City? Europe?

She smiled. "I hadn't gotten that far. But I've known deep down that this will be my last Christmas in Canyon Springs. It's too hard living in Dalton's shadow."

Cody tenderly took her hand in his. "I'm hoping together we can drive that shadow away, Paris."

A tingle of happiness raced through her. He hadn't rethought things in the hours since they'd parted last night. He hadn't changed his mind about them. "Me, too."

"Hey, Aunt Paris!" Deron called. "You gotta see this."

"Sounds as if you're being paged, *Aunt* Paris." An amused Cody squeezed her hand. As they stood, he glanced at his watch. "After you take a look at what he has to show you, we'll need to hit the road."

She sighed. "I'd hoped to see the houses you're flipping."

"I wish we had time to drive out to Trevor's folks' place, too, so you could meet them."

"Maybe another time?"

"That's a promise."

Before heading back to the mountains, they stopped for burgers and fries, enjoying the remaining warmth of the day from the restaurant's patio. Deron didn't sleep on the way home as she—and probably Cody—had hoped, so there was little opportunity for conversation of a more personal variety.

Was that a taste of parenthood?

As they topped the Rim, snowflakes danced hypnotically in their headlights and, once they ushered Deron into the trailer and his car seat was removed, Paris got behind the wheel. Cody slipped into the passenger seat beside her for a sweet good-night kiss, then she headed home with his admonition to call him when she got there safely.

Still flying high from their afternoon together, Paris pulled into the garage, made a brief call to Cody and then let herself in through the side door. Seeing him with Deron today, she had no doubt he'd make a great dad. He had infinite patience and encouraged the boy to talk and share his ideas, to explore things that interested him.

Still smiling, she'd barely stepped into the darkened kitchen when a stern voice reprimanded her.

"Just where have you been?"

Chapter Nineteen

"Dad!" Paris's fingers found the light switch, illuminating the space.

Her father stood in the doorway across the room, arms crossed and a look of disapproval on his face. "I've been worried about you."

"You didn't see my note?"

"I saw it. And I also got a call from someone saying they saw Cody Hawk driving your SUV and you sitting in the passenger seat."

Who'd ratted her out? Sometimes living in a small town was akin to having a camera trained on you every time you stepped out the door. She placed her purse on the kitchen table and peeled out of her coat, resigned that the time had come—earlier than she'd hoped—to have a heart-to-heart with her father.

"We went to the Valley to pick up his tux."

"What does he need a tuxedo for?" His expression was wary, as if suspecting the answer to his question.

"He's…" *Spit it out, Paris.* "My escort for the Christmas gala."

Her father shook his head. "Honey, we both know that isn't a good idea."

"Cody is *not* Leroy. He's nothing like his father or his brothers. He never was."

Dad stretched out his hand toward her. "You may have lived here your whole life, sweetheart, but there are things you don't know about those people. Things that are not nice."

"I'm aware of his half brothers' reputations. The auto theft. Drugs. Drinking. Illegitimate kids. But that's not Cody, Dad. He's nothing like them."

"You think not, but—"

"The apple," she quoted, "doesn't fall far from the tree?"

"There's considerable truth in that statement. More than you know."

"Cody's a God-believing man who's overcome his unfortunate background. A man with a kind and generous heart. A man who—"

Who loves me. A man I love.

Why couldn't she bring herself to say those words? To tell Dad the truth? But she didn't want to make him angry, to hurt him.

"I fully comprehend that Cody is the type of man who's undoubtedly caught the eye of many a lady through the years. But he has no business talking you into taking him to the gala and risking your reputation."

Paris endeavored to keep her voice even, respectful. "He didn't talk me into anything. I asked him to be my escort and it took considerable persuasion on my part for the same reason you're pointing out. He was concerned for me."

"Clever tactic."

"No, Dad, it wasn't a tactic. Cody cares for me."

Dad shot her an exasperated look. "Of course he does. You're a beautiful young woman. No doubt he 'cares' for your financial and social standing, as well. But if he thinks worming his way into the gala will fling open the doors of opportunity here in Canyon Springs, he's highly mistaken."

"He's not looking for opportunities in Canyon Springs. He's a businessman in Phoenix. A successful one."

"That's what he's telling you?"

"I believe him."

Dad held up his hand. "Regardless, I don't want you going to the gala with a Hawk. I love you, Paris. You know that. But you have no idea of the repercussions that will ensue if you persist in this."

A sharp retort on the tip of her tongue, her response nevertheless came softly. "For me—or for you?"

Her father drew in a sharp breath. "Parker Herrington will be in town this week and that's who will be escorting you."

She took a step toward her father. "Dad, please try to—"

"This discussion is over. Good night." He abruptly turned away and left her standing alone in the kitchen.

"Can I come, too, Uncle Cody?" Deron looked up from the breakfast table early Monday morning as he spooned up another bite of cereal, his dark eyes eager. "I can eat fast."

Cody zipped his jacket, then placed a hand on Deron's shoulder. "Not this morning, bud. I have a lot of work to do and there's no place there for little boys to play."

"I can play outside in the snow. I have boots."

"Now don't nag your uncle," Ma chided gently as she sat down across the table from her step-grandson.

She smiled at Cody, obviously pleased that Deron continued to warm up to him. He seemed to be adjusting better than expected, soaking up the attention they gave to him. It would be good to get him in school, but local education officials still awaited the records Carson had promised. So it would again be a half day with Ma and a half day with the neighbor.

It was still dark when Cody headed to his truck, his thoughts drifting, as always, to Paris. He never would have dreamed when he'd wakened on Saturday morning that by evening he'd have her in his arms.

"She loves me, Lord." With a chuckle, he shook his head as he slipped behind the steering wheel. Although they hadn't much time for conversation with Deron aboard Sunday afternoon, their shared smiles that had sent his heart soaring proved she hadn't changed her mind. And yet...

They were meeting for lunch today, but why did he feel as if the other shoe was yet to drop? God orchestrated this unexpected turn of events, yet he found himself afraid to revel in it for fear of it being snatched away.

What kind of ungrateful slob was he, anyway? How would he feel if Deron wouldn't wear his new coat and boots for fear his uncle would grab them back? Cody let out a gust of pent-up breath and started the engine.

"I trust You, Lord. Forgive my unbelief."

Backing to the end of the driveway, he abruptly slammed on the brakes as his back-up lights illuminated a dark SUV pulling across the base of the drive, blocking his way. What in the—?

His heart jerked with recognition. A Lexus. Cody cut the engine and stepped out of the truck, doubting Mr. Perslow was here to welcome him into the family.

Merle left his vehicle running, its headlights

cutting a swath down the graveled road, but he stepped out to join Cody in front of his SUV.

Cody rammed his hands into his jacket pockets. "I take it this isn't a social call."

"How much, Hawk?" Merle pulled out his wallet and opened it, his hand poised above a thick wad of bills.

"I don't understand."

"How much will it take to get you out of my daughter's life?" He motioned to his wallet. "There's more where this came from. Let's settle this once and for all. No more nickel-and-diming."

What was he rattling on about? "I don't want your money, Mr. Perslow."

"No? But the bottom line is Paris isn't yours for the taking. I thought I made that clear. I'll protect her no matter what, so name your price." Merle's eyes narrowed in an uncompromising glare. "Make no mistake, you and yours will not be allowed to prey on my innocent daughter. I won't have her involved in the games Hawks play. You got that?"

A ripple of uneasiness clawed its way up the back of Cody's neck. There was that reference again to Hawks playing games. And what was that "nickel-and-diming" allusion?

Leroy.

"I don't know what you're talking about. I care deeply for your daughter. I think you know I always have."

"You're telling me you *love* her?" Merle made a scoffing sound. "I'll concede the fact that you've always *wanted* her, but love? The only Hawk who knows anything about love may be your mother and even that might be a stretch."

Cody held his tongue. How much had Paris told her father about them? That he was her escort for the gala—or everything?

Merle waved his wallet. "Let's get this over with. How much?"

"I told you," Cody said, stepping away from the vehicle, "I won't take your money."

The older man's lips tightened as he rammed the billfold into his back pocket. "Just remember, Hawk, you'll be sorry if you show up at the gala with my daughter. Real sorry."

Paris's father got back into his Lexus and Cody stared after the SUV as it headed down the road. There was nothing Mr. Perslow could do that would make him disappoint Paris by backing out of the gala. She'd take it that he didn't trust her, didn't believe in her love. But he had no doubt Paris's father, although misguided, cared for his daughter. How could he win the man's trust? How could he make him understand that he loved her, too?

But Merle had made several points that were more than disturbing. As much as Cody needed to push ahead, his work on the Christmas gala would have to wait.

It was time to pay another visit to Leroy Hawk.

* * *

"I'm sorry, Elizabeth, but I'm not going to the gala with Parker." Hoping for a sign of support, Paris glanced across her bedroom to where Delaney stood holding the gown Elizabeth had delivered that morning. A slight nod bolstered her determination to stand her ground.

"But *Cody Hawk?*" Dalton's mother stared at her, aghast. "Sweetie, you can't show up with him. Your reputation will be in shreds before you're even seated." Elizabeth appealed to Delaney, her eyes beseeching. "You're her best friend. Tell her I'm speaking the truth."

"I think," Delaney said gently, "that you're speaking the truth as you know it and that you have Paris's best at heart. But when two people are in love—"

Elizabeth gasped and spun toward Paris. "*Love?* What is she talking about? Don't tell me this Hawk has convinced you he's in love with you."

"He not only loves me, but I love him, too."

"Oh, my—" Shaken, Elizabeth lowered herself to Paris's bed. "Surely you're not intending to marry a son of Leroy Hawk?"

He hadn't proposed in so many words, but the expectation was there, wasn't it? "We haven't made any decisions yet."

"Marriage or not, I can't imagine your father approves of any of this. A Hawk escorting you. Dating you."

"He will. Eventually." But doubt crept in. She'd read that morning in *Dear Abby* about a family that cut off contact with a grown son due to his choice in a marriage partner. But Dad wouldn't do that to her, his only child, would he?

Elizabeth motioned helplessly. "Sweetie, I know you were badly hurt when Dalton died, that you've been lonely. I've only recently come to realize that, which is why I've encouraged you to see Parker. But there are any number of young men who would be vastly more suitable than Cody Hawk. Don't do this to yourself. Nothing good can come of it."

The two women stared at each other, Elizabeth in obvious anguish and Paris's heart torn asunder. She knew, had always known, that caring for Cody Hawk would carry a price. But Dad...and now Elizabeth, who'd always been like a second mother to her? Would neither support her and Cody together?

"We've cared for each other ever since we were kids." Paris pressed her hand to her heart. "I know in here that it's right. That God's in it."

Elizabeth rose, tears pricking her eyes. "You're saying you were in love with this man when you promised to marry my son?"

"No, no, I mean—"

Elizabeth waved her off and moved to the hallway door, then turned with sorrowful eyes. "Please don't tarnish Dalton's memory, Paris. Don't drag my son's name into the mire to be forever associated with a woman who gave herself to a Hawk."

She disappeared out the door and Paris drew a shaky breath as her gaze met Delaney's. "That went well, didn't it? I didn't mean to upset her like that."

Her friend slipped the gown's hanger over a hook on the closet door, then smoothed the velvet skirt. "You'd have to tell her sometime."

"I know, but—"

"She loves you, Paris. She'll always love Dalton. Losing you now to someone who isn't her son, regardless of whether it's to Cody or another man, is like losing Dalton all over again. That's how closely the two of you are entwined in her heart."

"Maybe Cody is right, then? Going to the gala together is too much too soon?"

Her friend approached with a determined look. "You love him, right?"

"I do. I think a part of me always has."

"And he loves you. There's no shame in letting the world know of the happiness God's brought into your life."

Paris sat on the bed, the heaviness in her heart weighing her down. "But all it's bringing into the lives of others I love is hurt and anger and disappointment with me. Surely that can't be of God."

"God's ways are not always our ways, Paris. Maybe there are lessons He wants them to learn here, too."

"But it's bad enough that Dad's angry Cody will be escorting me. He's going to be furious if Elizabeth tells him how I truly feel about him."

Delaney folded her arms. "And what if he is? You have to be prepared for that. That is, unless Elizabeth and your father are making you rethink things...?"

"No. Never."

"Well then? Once they see how happy Cody makes you, once they come to know him and the kind of man that he is, how could they object? It may take a little time—or maybe a lot. But mostly you need to be certain that God's in this, that you're not—as Elizabeth implied—merely longing for a replacement for Dalton and any man will do."

"Cody isn't *any* man, Delaney," she said more sharply than intended.

"I didn't think so." Her friend smiled, not taking offense.

"You've met him, but I want you to spend time with him, to get to know him. I want you to recognize for yourself what an amazing man he is. How God has worked in his life."

Delaney rolled her eyes. "Spending time with Cody will be such a hardship."

"So, you don't think I'm making a mistake?"

Delaney gently grasped Paris's upper arms and, drawing her to her feet, looked her square in the eye. "I told my mother I've never seen you so happy in all the years I've known you. Does that sound like I think you're making a mistake?"

Joy bubbled as Paris hugged her friend, remembering she was to have lunch with the love of her life today.

And yet…a nagging voice still questioned.

Would Cody think it was a mistake if her friends and family cut them off—or when he thought about spending a lifetime of holidays in their disapproving midst?

Chapter Twenty

"Look, Dad, Mr. Perslow made strong insinuations about 'games Hawks play.' He brought up being 'nickeled-and-dimed' and told me flat out that 'you and yours' won't be allowed to prey on his innocent daughter."

"Still trying…get hands on her?" What sounded like a chuckle emanated from his father's misshapen lips. "Pretty gal, ain't she?"

Irritated for inadvertently bringing Paris into the conversation, Cody didn't respond.

"Ain't she?" Dad said more forcefully. "And you…want…bad."

Cody had no intention of discussing his relationship with Paris with his father. Like Ma, Dad had recognized Cody's interest in Paris many years ago, but his commentary had always been mocking of Cody, disrespectful and suggestive. He didn't like that then and he'd have none of it now.

Dad snorted, amusement lighting his eyes as he

motioned for Cody to come closer. "Can get her… for you, son."

Cody stood rooted to the floor. "What do you mean?"

"Her daddy…" His father smirked. "Ain't what… pretends…be."

He tensed as his worst fear took deeper root. The "nickel-and-diming" reference Paris's father had made was too reminiscent of what he'd remembered as a boy from one of his dad's incarcerations.

Extortion.

He took a steadying breath. "What do you think he's pretending to be?"

"Faithful family man." Dad gave a lame attempt at a leering wink. "But extra… Extracurricular… activity on side."

A knot tightened in Cody's chest. Paris's adored father, a church deacon, was having an intimate relationship with someone outside of marriage?

"You've been blackmailing Merle Perslow."

Dad shrugged, a sly smile tugging at his lips. "Job…security."

No wonder Paris's father met him with hostility upon his return to Canyon Springs. Looking back at each of their encounters, it was clear he had it in his head that Cody was a part of this, too.

Dad bought a new truck a few years ago. That was likely the start of it and he'd been "nickel-and-diming" Merle ever since. He'd have derived immense enjoyment from it. "For how long?"

The older man squinted, thinking back. "Fifteen...years?"

Fifteen years? Paris's mother would still have been alive. Merle had cheated on Marna Perslow? The saintly woman who'd given so much of herself to her husband and daughter and the community?

"I don't believe you." But as much as he didn't want to, there had to be truth to it. A man like Merle Perslow wouldn't succumb to blackmail easily. There had to be evidence. Something concrete. Cody had to get his hands on it.

Dad's eyes narrowed. "Photos...can prove."

"I want to see them."

Dad's chuckle turned into a deep, rasping cough and his face reddened.

Cody reached for the water glass on the bedside table, but his dad waved him off with his good hand. He coughed a few more times, then slid himself down from where Cody had earlier propped him on a pillow.

"You go...now."

He was being dismissed? Just like that? "Where are the photos, Dad?"

The older man turned away, his mumbling voice barely audible. "For me...know."

And for you to find out?

"I've got to get going, Paris. I had to run an errand and got behind on things at the clubhouse."

Paris sensed Cody's restlessness as he glanced

out the front window of Camilla's Café for what had to be the hundredth time. He'd been late meeting her and seemed on edge throughout their meal. Was being seen with her in a public place making him nervous? If lunch could do that, what would happen at the gala a few nights from now?

"Are you having second thoughts about escorting me?" She hadn't breathed a word about her encounters with Dad and Elizabeth, hoping the turmoil would resolve itself soon. There was no point in giving Cody any excuses to back out.

He didn't meet her gaze as he paused to take a sip from his water glass. "No, of course not."

"Because if you are…"

"Nope. Not me. What about you?"

"I'm looking forward to it." She'd leaped the highest hurdles by telling Dad and Elizabeth she'd be going to the gala with him. "Is everything okay? You seem distracted."

He placed his glass back on the table. "I have a lot on my mind."

"Is it anything it would help to share with me?"

He cut her a sharp look that immediately softened. "I'm concerned about Deron. And Dad and Ma. I need to get this project behind me so I can focus on their issues and my company."

And on the two of them? Had it only been a few days ago that they'd first opened their hearts and tentatively talked about a shared future?

"Were the volunteers there to decorate the trees

this morning?" She folded her hands on the table. "I haven't had time to stop by."

"What? Oh. I assume so. I haven't been out there yet. Like I told you, I had an errand to run. In Show Low."

"To see your Dad?"

"Right."

Calling his father an "errand" seemed odd, proving that something was troubling him.

"Are you going straight to Pine Shadow Ridge from here? I was thinking maybe we—"

"I have another thing or two to attend to first." Apparently recognizing the vagueness of his excuse, he offered a reassuring smile and reached across the table to take her hand in his. "Maybe we can get together tonight? A late dinner?"

"I can't. I'm meeting with Abby and Brett at Kit's to finalize the catering for their Friday-evening wedding."

"Tomorrow night, then?"

"Choir practice."

"Wednesday?"

"A gift exchange at the office." She sighed, then perked up. "Would you like to come?"

"I doubt your father would care to have me there." He ran his thumb across the back of her hand. "I'm assuming, of course, he now knows we're seeing each other? You haven't mentioned how that went."

"He knows we'll be at the gala together." Should

she confess to Cody that she hadn't yet told Dad their relationship was much deeper than attendance at a charity event?

A crease furrowed Cody's forehead. "How'd he take that?"

"He wasn't happy. But Delaney assures me that once he gets to know you, he'll come around."

"Your friend's an optimistic soul."

Paris smiled. "Always."

Cody gave her hand a gentle squeeze, then stood. "I'll give you a call later."

But he didn't say when.

It was with a sense of foreboding that Paris watched him pause at the cashier, then push open the glass-paned door. Snowflakes filled the air, swirling around him. Yes, it was beginning to look a lot like Christmas.

But it sure didn't feel like it.

Cody stood in deep shadow outside the clubhouse Saturday night, oblivious of the cold for which his tux provided little defense. He and Paris had taken separate vehicles since she needed to come early to meet with the committee, caterers and staff. But in a matter of minutes he'd join the continuous stream of arriving guests and step through the doors to meet her at the agreed-upon time.

Right now, though, he needed to find his bearings. It had been a rough week, starting with Dad's sickening revelation about Mr. Perslow and fearing each time he spoke with Paris that she could read his every anxious thought—every spark of anger directed at her father and his own.

Fifteen years ago, Dad wouldn't have had a digital camera. He still didn't own one. But where would he have stashed the incriminating photos *and their negatives?* Repeated searches of the garage and trailer had left Cody empty-handed. That the photos were incriminating, he had no doubt. Merle Perslow was smart enough to know Leroy Hawk could shout his accusations from the rooftops and no one would listen to a word he said.

Unless he had rock-solid evidence.

Knowing what he did about her father had made Cody uncomfortable around Paris the past several days. She sensed it and he could tell it confused her. But until he found those photographs and destroyed them, he'd feel part of Leroy Hawk's vindictive scheme and her father's infidelity.

Cody glanced skyward into the star-filled night—a night like the one when he'd first kissed Paris. Would he ever be able to bring himself to tell her the truth? Or would this ugliness stand between them for a lifetime?

Please, Lord, don't let my coming to this event cause negative repercussions for Paris.

He waited a few minutes more, allowing the stragglers to enter, then squared his shoulders and went inside. Now, standing in the foyer and looking down at a beautifully gowned Paris, his spirits rose. God was in this. Everything would be okay.

"I'm sorry I was tied up with the wedding last night, but I'm glad you brought your mother to see her design come to life." Her hair piled atop her head and earrings sparkling, Paris smiled up at him. "What are she and Deron doing tonight?"

"Ma's at a gathering with her Bible study group and her next-door neighbor is keeping Deron. The kids were out in the front yard building a snowman when I left."

Paris's brow wrinkled. "What's going to happen to him, Cody?"

"I don't know. But I'll tell you one thing—if Dad ever comes home, I can't leave the little guy there. Dad might not be able to swing his fist like he used to, but he could still do emotional damage."

"I can't understand why I promised never to tell anyone about the way he treated you. What kind of friend was I?"

He looked into her troubled eyes. "We were only kids, Paris. That's in the past now. But, whatever it takes, I won't let Dad's temper ruin the future of another child."

She glanced around to make sure no one was watching, then stepped up on her tiptoes to kiss him on the cheek.

He grinned. "What was that for?"

"For being the most loving, kindhearted man I've ever known."

He straightened his bow tie. "And the most handsome?"

"Definitely. I'll be keeping an eye on you tonight so none of the other ladies attempt to steal you away from me."

"There will only be one woman in there who I'm interested in." He offered his arm to her. "So are you ready to set the tongues wagging?"

"I am if you are." She linked her arm with his and together, with bated breath, they entered the ballroom.

It was probably his imagination that the room fell silent when they stepped into the raftered space that had been transformed into a rustic winter wonderland. It was probably all in his head, too, that the hush was swiftly followed by a soft buzz as guests turned to whisper to their tablemates.

Nevertheless, he nodded a warm greeting to those they passed on the way to their reserved table near the front of the elevated stage, reminding himself that the beautiful woman on his arm had chosen him, out of all the men on the planet, to join her tonight.

Black-and-red buffalo plaid tablecloths topped with glass-encased candles set a mellow mood with the overhead lights dimmed. An open space in the middle of the room would serve as an after-dinner dance floor.

"Cody." Bill Diaz rose from his seat to shake hands as they passed by. "Good to see you. You, too, Paris."

"The decorations are out of this world," Sharon Dixon chimed in. "Absolutely breathtaking."

"They are, aren't they?" Paris smiled up at him, her eyes shining.

"So this is the young man responsible for this magnificent craftsmanship?" Former city councilman Reuben Falkner stepped forward. For a moment Cody hesitated. Mr. Falkner had more than once chased him off when he'd taken a shortcut home from school through his property.

Cody shook his hand, only to be tapped on the shoulder and drawn into another conversation praising his and his mother's work. Astoundingly, the warm welcomes continued as they wound their way among the tables. Only a few times did he catch a fleeting frown or see someone deliberately turn away from them.

Owen looked disgruntled, but managed not to sneer.

All too soon, however, they arrived at tables reserved for those who'd played a major role in making the Christmas gala the charity event of the year. Among them, one table away from where he and Paris were to be seated, was an exquisitely dressed Elizabeth Herrington and her escort for the evening, Paris's father.

Elizabeth and Merle. A cold, invisible finger

pressed against Cody's spine. Would hers be the face he'd see in the photographs Dad stashed away? The woman Paris loved like a second mother? No, it couldn't be. On top of her father's betrayal of her mother, that would be too cruel.

Mrs. Herrington nodded regally, too well-bred to publicly shun him, but Mr. Perslow didn't rise to shake his hand like the other men at the table did.

To his relief, he and Paris were seated with their backs to Elizabeth and Merle. But he could still feel the man's steely gray eyes boring into his back, a reminder of his promise that Cody would be sorry if he appeared at the event with Paris.

However, the evening was off to a promising start, with Paris and her committee extending a formal welcome to the guests and thanking them for their generous donations that would sustain community charities throughout the year.

Throughout dinner, he joined the conversation around the table, answering questions about the creation of his mother's decorative designs. It was gratifying as well to share details regarding his and Trevor's business expansion and several at the table expressed interest in learning more about a possible investment of their own.

"Didn't I tell you everything would be fine?" Paris whispered in his ear.

"You did. And—" he whispered back, unable to keep from teasing her "—I haven't felt the least bit neglected by the gala's committee head. Not long ago I thought I overheard her insisting she wouldn't have time to deal with an escort."

"I already told you what my responsibilities for the evening are." She gave him a playful smile. "Keeping at bay the women who have their eye on you."

He grinned, nodding to the band members gearing up for after-dinner dancing. "Maybe I can bribe them to play only slow numbers."

She nodded at him with approval and his heart rate ramped up a notch. Being seated here by Paris, announcing to the world they were a couple...it still didn't seem real. He turned toward the front of the ballroom where dozens of the high-school-aged waiters and waitresses converged on the stage piling festively wrapped boxes and pushing beribboned scooters, go-carts and bicycles.

"What's this?" he whispered to Paris as an unwelcome memory pricked his mind.

"They're displaying the gifts that will be distributed to children in the community."

He nodded, relieved—until he heard high-pitched, childish chatter at the back of the ballroom. His muscles tensed as he turned in that direction. In the dim light he could see two dozen giggling grade-school-aged children moving restlessly just inside the main double doors, some hopping from one foot to another in excitement.

Cody reached for Paris's hand, his gaze piercing into hers. "You said they didn't do this anymore."

"I—"

"Children!" Sharlene Odel called from the stage microphone, drawing Cody's attention as a knot formed in his throat. "Please join me up here."

With giggles and whispers, the kids quickly wove their way among the tables. But Cody wasn't seeing them, was barely aware of Paris's hand gripping his as a familiar, humiliating warmth crept up his neck.

His mouth going dry, Cody pulled his hand free of Paris's and reached for his water glass. Was it his imagination, or were people staring at him, remembering he'd been paraded to the front with the other needy children in the past, being reminded that he had no business here among them and certainly not at Paris's side?

He didn't dare meet their gazes but kept his eyes trained on Sharlene, who was rambling on about the generosity of those assembled tonight.

In an effort to still his hammering heart, he prayed for every child crowded on the stage, focusing on each youthful face. Some were bursting with excitement, eyes dancing. Others appeared shy, withdrawn. Or embarrassed. He prayed they'd hold their heads up proudly. Prayed they had a family who loved them and who shared God's love with them. Prayed they'd one day break out of the cycle of poverty.

There was no shame in being poor—Jesus had been far from rich—but there *was* shame in looking down on the impoverished, using them for entertainment. How could Paris have allowed this spectacle when she knew how he hated it?

Pausing on each face as his gaze slowly made its prayerful way through the throng on the stage, he was barely aware of Sharlene's words.

And then, as his eyes touched on a familiar boyish face, an invisible fist punched him in the gut. A blow that would have brought him to his knees had he been standing.

Deron.

There. At the far left side. At the back. Smiling uncertainly. Looking a little scared.

No. No. Please, Lord, no!

Instinctively, Cody rose to his feet. Paris grasped his arm in an effort to restrain him, but he shook her off. Looking neither left nor right, he strode to the stage and, to Sharlene's surprise, stepped up onto the platform. In a blink of an eye, he had Deron in his arms and headed toward a side door.

He only paused once to look back—into Paris's guilt-stricken eyes. And at Merle's smirking mouth.

"Where are we going, Uncle Cody?" Deron looped his arm around Cody's neck as they strode into the starry night. "The man said I could have a bicycle."

The man. Merle?

How could You have let Paris be a part of this, Lord?

"I'll get you a bicycle, Deron." His heart aching, he gave the boy a hug. "The biggest and best bicycle in the whole wide world."

Chapter Twenty-One

"Sit down and don't make a scene," her father's low voice warned as Paris tried to slip past him in pursuit of Cody, his grip on her wrist tightening. "There's been enough of that tonight. I hope you're happy."

Waves of icy cold flushed through her from the moment she'd spied Deron. Had her father played a role in staging this humiliation of Cody and his family?

She should have known something like this would happen. But Dad was right. She couldn't abandon the gala to chase after Cody, no matter how much she wanted to. From the look he'd leveled on her from across the dimly lit room, he wouldn't be in any mood to listen to anything she had to say anyway. He blamed her. And rightly so, if Dad had anything to do with this.

When Cody had stepped off the stage, Sharlene immediately drew the guests' attention to the excited children as she gave the go-ahead to open presents. Grateful for the continued distraction, Paris numbly returned to her seat to the sound of happy squeals and tearing wrapping paper.

Please, God, be with Cody. Please let him forgive me.

The remainder of the evening was a blur. As soon as the packages were opened, the band struck up a popular Christmas tune and couples milled onto the dance floor. Parker appeared out of nowhere to sweep her into dance after dance and others cut in throughout the night, including Bill Diaz, who was one of several who told her not to worry about what happened with Cody, assuring her everything would be all right.

If only she could believe that.

Dad didn't approach her to dance their traditional dance together. That was evidence enough of his guilt, wasn't it? Or was he merely angry with her because Cody had disrupted the evening? Perslows did *not* make scenes.

When late in the evening the band's final song came to a close, she and the other committee members stepped to the microphone to thank everyone for coming and wished them a merry Christmas. Others were in charge of overseeing breakdown and cleanup, so as soon as she could, she made her escape.

But she'd no more than stepped into the softly lit hallway that surrounded three sides of the ballroom when she saw Elizabeth standing off to the side. Shoulders slumped, she leaned against a window frame, staring out the floor-to-ceiling glass expanse and into the night.

As if sensing Paris's presence, she turned a tearstained face toward her. With only a slight hesitation, she stretched out her hand to beckon Paris closer and, when she approached, clasped Paris's hand tightly.

"I'm so very sorry. This is my fault and I can no longer carry the burden of what I've done to you—and Dalton."

Dalton? "I…don't understand."

She tilted her head to gaze lovingly at Paris, blinking back tears. "No, no, you wouldn't. And when I tell you, you may never speak to me again."

"Elizabeth—"

"Hear me out. Please? From where I sat tonight I could catch glimpses of you throughout dinner, see the glow in your eyes when you looked at Cody. Hear the sparkle in your laugh. And suddenly I realized you really *do* love him."

"I do."

"He looked at you the same way, with respect and a gentle protectiveness." Elizabeth took a breath. "I know you've been lonely. I know I— and everyone else in town—remind you all too often of Dalton and haven't allowed you to move beyond your grief."

Why would she think Paris would never want

to speak to her if that was her only confession? "Elizabeth—"

The weary-looking woman held up her hand to again halt Paris. "What I'm trying to say is...it's *my* fault that you lost Dalton."

Paris shook her head, not understanding any of this.

"Oh, sweetheart." Another tear trickled down the carefully made-up cheeks. "You see, I pressured Dalton to return home earlier than planned for the wedding."

A chill coursed through Paris.

"I'd filled the week with gatherings that would showcase *me* as the mother of the groom," Elizabeth rushed on. "I insisted he be here for them so I could show off the both of you. Make me look and feel important. He finally gave in to my persistence, to my sometimes angry haranguing. And...and it brought my dear boy home. Right into the path of a drunken driver."

Cody let the neighbor next door know he'd picked up Deron and got confirmation that, as when he'd been a kid, a rented bus had made its way through the neighborhood with gala volunteers knocking on doors and gathering children. Then he changed clothes, plugged in the lights on the tabletop tree they'd gotten for Deron and played a few board games with him.

But his mind wasn't on games.

"I like this popcorn, don't you, Uncle Cody?"

He ruffled the boy's hair and helped himself to the tin of caramel-covered popcorn. "Yeah. It's good."

He shouldn't have gone charging onto the stage. Maybe no one would have noticed a grandson of Leroy Hawk—who bore a striking resemblance to his uncle Cody. But he had been hurtled back in time, seeing himself standing there in front of the crowd with everyone staring, knowing he was Leroy's son, knowing he'd come for a handout.

Had Paris known they were going to resurrect the old custom? She hadn't denied it. But then again, he hadn't given her much of a chance before he'd shaken off her hand. In his first—and now-to-be-only—foray into Canyon Springs society, he'd hauled Deron off the stage, no doubt embarrassing Paris. To top it off, he'd not only humiliated her in front of her family and friends, he'd left her dateless for the remainder of the evening.

At the mercy of Parker and Owen.

"It's your turn, Uncle Cody."

"Oh, sorry, bud." He drew a printed card from the stack, then moved his playing piece forward on the game board.

Why'd he think he could fit in with that crowd anyway? He'd only been fooling himself. He'd be forever tainted in this town by his former poverty, his father's and brothers' reputations, and the shadow of the blackmailing of Mr. Perslow. By his own disastrous public performance tonight, as well. That should give the community's elite something to whisper about…and to negatively judge Paris for inviting him.

With the gala over, though, he was free to leave town and release Paris from any sense of obligation. If only he could find those photos, destroy them and somehow destroy the guilt by association that haunted him. It wouldn't make any difference in his doomed-from-the-start relationship with Paris, but he couldn't allow Dad to feather his own nest at the expense of another man's dishonorable deed.

The rattle of the front door announced his mother's return. Cody used the opportunity to communicate a silent "later" shake of his head, then he wrapped up his game with Deron and slipped out to the garage to resume his search for the evidence. He combed the rafters once more, pulled out drawers looking for anything taped to them and dug through bins of nails, screws and whatever else he could lay his hands on.

He *had* to find and destroy the photos and negatives—for Paris. That's the least he could do after what he'd done to her tonight.

But an hour's worth of effort was to no avail.

Defeated, he paused in the doorway, his hand on the light switch as he gave the workbench a final sweeping glance. The pegboard filled with tools. The jars and bins lined up. The hodgepodge of key chains and their shiny metal keys looped over hooks...

In a flash he was at the workbench, spreading out the handful of keys and studying their varied key chains. Most were likely freebies. Advertising for a local insurance company. The grain and feed store. A self-storage facility...

He picked up that one and studied it—a business in neighboring Hunter Ridge, about thirty minutes from Canyon Springs. The key chain was likely another promo item and the heavy-duty key dangling from it unrelated. But then again...where did Dad keep his boat? It wasn't on the property at the trailer, and he distinctly remembered Ma mentioning Dad had gone out on Casey Lake one last time for the season early in November.

Cody clenched the key in his hand.

Please, Lord, let this be it.

It was after midnight when Paris, still reeling from Cody's abrupt departure and Elizabeth's confession, let herself into the house. She'd attempted to call Cody several times throughout the evening, but he didn't pick up nor did he respond to her text messages. And now, standing in Dad's study as he defended his actions, she could only stare in numb disbelief.

"Blackmail? Cody is *blackmailing* you?"

Her father paced the floor in front of the fireplace. "I didn't want to tell you, honey, but it's clear you'd never believe what I've been telling you all along about Hawks. They're bad news. Tonight was my way of publicly letting Cody know I'm standing my ground. I refuse to live any longer in fear of his and his father's intimidation."

"But Dad—"

Her father drew to a halt, his irate gaze fixed on her. "No matter the cost to myself, to my own reputation, I'm not going to give in to demands that place my daughter in the middle of their schemes."

Paris rounded the brightly lit Christmas tree and crossed the room to lay a comforting hand on his arm. "I know you're upset, but I'm not understanding any of this. What am I in the middle of? And what could you possibly be blackmailed for?"

Sometimes Dad drove a hard bargain, skated as close to the edge as the law allowed, but he always kept things aboveboard.

"The less you know, the better." He pulled away and moved to stand behind his desk. "Suffice it to say I made bad choices and, unfortunately, Leroy Hawk was witness to them. He's been toying with me—like a cat pulling the legs off a bug, one by one, getting his kicks out of making periodic demands and watching me squirm. Well, I'm squirming no more."

He slammed his fist on the desk, rattling the pen-filled cup holder she'd made for him in grade school.

"But what's this have to do with Cody and me?"

None of this made any sense and certainly not the part about Cody playing a part in it.

"Don't you see? Leroy's out of commission and suddenly Cody's in town to pick up where his father left off. Only he's not demanding money, but demanding *you*." He raised his brows at Paris's sound of protest. "He's always wanted you, but he'll have you over my dead body."

"I told you, Cody cares for me. And I care for him, too."

With anguish-filled eyes, her father came from around the desk to take her hands in his. "He's using you to get back at me. He thinks my reputation, the respect of my family and community, means more to me than you do. But he's wrong."

"No, Dad. He loves me and—" she took a deep breath, garnering strength to meet her father's gaze "—I love him."

His grip tightened. "I know you *think* you do. I know he's convinced you he does. But honey, you have to listen to me. You have to know that if I could do things over again, if I could go back in time and make better choices, I would. No matter what happens, no matter what you might hear, you have to believe that."

She pulled away from him. "Cody wouldn't blackmail you. He wouldn't blackmail anyone."

A pitying gaze met hers. "I know you don't want to believe he's involved in this sordid business. I wish he wasn't. But he's trying to coerce me to hand over my reputation—or my daughter. He's gambling that my standing in the community, my good name, will win out and I'll give my blessing to his pursuit of you. But that will *not* happen. I love you too much."

If only she could get in touch with Cody. If only he could explain to her what was going on. Did his refusal to respond to her phone calls mean Dad was right? That he—and Leroy—recognized by what happened at the gala that her father was no longer willing to go along with extortion? So Cody had made himself scarce?

No. While she didn't doubt Leroy could be involved in blackmail, she refused to believe Cody was using it to force Dad to sanction a relationship with her.

Her father took a hesitant step closer. "I'm sorry to tell you like this, but I tried every way I could think of to avoid it. I've given Cody plenty of opportunities to back off."

A sliver of cold crept up the back of her neck. Why had Cody not said anything to her? Could that mean…? "You talked to Cody about this?"

"Several times. But I'm not taking it anymore. I'm not proud of what I did, but this has gone on long enough."

Paris moved behind a wingback chair, gripping the back of it as if to draw courage. *What's going on, Lord?*

"If this involves Cody and me, don't you think I have a right to know *why* you're being black-mailed?"

Her father's pain-filled eyes met hers, indecision flickering. Her hopes sank that he might be over-dramatizing, blowing a minor indiscretion out of proportion.

"Please, Dad?"

He lowered himself into the chair in front of her, bracing his elbows on his knees and placing his head in his hands. The clock on the fireplace mantel ticked away the seconds echoing in the silence.

And then came a sob.

Struggling to breathe, she stared down at her father's bowed head and shaking shoulders. What had he done that would bring him to this broken-ness? She moved to the side of the chair and knelt down to place a hand on his arm. "Dad?"

He drew a resigned breath, then turned tear-filled eyes to her. "I…I had an affair with a married woman."

Paris swallowed. *Elizabeth?* Her husband had died only five years ago. Had Dad, in his loneli-ness—? But Paris couldn't bring herself to ask. She didn't want to know.

"I'm sorry, sweetheart." His words came in a breathless rasp. "Can you ever forgive me?"

Aching deep inside as the father she loved fell from the pedestal she'd placed him on long ago, her heart nevertheless filled with compassion. She reached out to pull him into her arms, cradled and soothed him as she would a child.

Clearly, though, her father's shocking revelation was worthy of extortion and its exposure would impact his standing in the community, the church, his business.

That Leroy would take advantage of a situation like that, she had no doubt.

But please, God, not Cody, too.

Chapter Twenty-Two

On Monday afternoon, a brown envelope gripped in Cody's hands, the housekeeper admitted him into the Perslow's spacious home.

Paris hadn't tried to call him since the pleading messages of apology she'd left Saturday night, nor had he returned them. He intended to make his own apology face-to-face to make clear why a shared future was no longer possible. But the issues remaining to be resolved took precedence. Today he'd waited and watched until she returned to the office after lunch, then took his chances that her father might still be at home.

Yesterday afternoon he'd traveled to Hunter Ridge and at long last found the items he'd almost given up hope of finding. Initially he thought he'd once again come up empty-handed. But a prolonged search produced a zip-type plastic bag taped under a seat of Dad's fishing boat—a packet of photos and negatives identified with a discount store photo department in the Valley. Not surprisingly, Dad hadn't taken any chances having them developed anywhere nearby or delivered through the mail.

Yes, the photos were compromising, although not explicit. They caught Merle and his lady love entwined in each other's arms just inside the entrance to what appeared to be a remote cabin location. Innocent enough until you realized they weren't of him and his wife, and considered the date they were developed—a year before Marna Perslow's passing.

Even now, preparing to face Paris's father, he was filled with disgust. That anyone would cheat on Paris's mother and break vows taken before God was beyond his understanding.

"This way, Mr. Hawk," the housekeeper said when she returned to the foyer and motioned for him to follow.

When he stepped into the rustically appointed study, the housekeeper announced she was leaving for the day, then discreetly departed. Merle Perslow sat in a wingback chair next to the stone fireplace, its cheerful, welcoming crackle and the Christmas tree's bright points of light contrasting with the grim nature of Cody's visit.

Elbows propped on the arms of the chair and fingers tented, Paris's father acknowledged his presence with a nod. "Do come in and have a seat, Mr. Hawk. I've been expecting you."

Cody approached, but didn't sit down. "I won't

be here long. Only long enough to drop off something I think you might like to have."

He tossed the brown envelope to the coffee table and caught Merle's flinch, the tightening of his jaw.

Yesterday he'd come close to destroying the contents of the packet. What purpose would keeping it serve? But this morning, while Ma was enrolling Deron in school, he'd traveled to the hospital to show his father the evidence that his blackmailing days were over.

Dad hadn't been happy. He'd cussed out his son as best he could manage given his difficulties with speech, but he'd made his feelings clear. So another wall for God to tear down, a bridge to rebuild. If there was time.

On the drive back to Canyon Springs, though, Cody realized there might be legal ramifications for blackmailing Merle. Deciding what to do with the evidence used against Paris's father wasn't up to Cody.

It was Mr. Perslow's call.

Merle motioned to the packet. "I'm familiar with what I imagine you've brought to share with me. But no matter. I'm done with your and your father's manipulation. So don't expect to march in here and demand a blessing on a relationship with my daughter. There won't be one."

"I didn't imagine there would be." Cody held little hope that once Paris knew of his father's extortion that she'd want anything to do with Leroy's son. It was a nice dream while it had lasted, but clearly Hawks and Perslows weren't destined to make a match.

Merle snorted. "Then what are you doing here?"

"I'm returning personal photographs—and negatives—that someone of our mutual acquaintance has held in…safekeeping."

The older man's eyes narrowed. "Why would you do that?"

Cody stepped to the fireplace to look down into the dancing flames, then glanced at Paris's father. "There seems to be a serious misunderstanding between us. A misconception on your part. I've had nothing to do with the extortion my father has been involved in."

Merle motioned to the envelope. "Don't you think *this* in your possession contradicts such a statement?"

Not surprisingly, Mr. Perlsow wouldn't be easy to convince.

"Things you recently said led me to confront my father with my suspicions. It took some doing, but I tracked down the proof of what he shared with me, what he's been holding over your head. It's up to you what you do with it. I want no part of this ugliness."

"You expect me to believe these are the only copies?"

"It's my sincere belief that they are. But regardless, if you decide to press charges against my father, I'll testify on your behalf."

Merle stood, his expression uncertain. "Is this for real, Hawk?"

"It is." Cody folded his arms. "Make no mistake, Mr. Perslow, while I don't condone what you did, I have a feeling you've paid a heavy price for your wrongdoing. But I wasn't aware of what my dad was up to until a few days ago. I've had nothing to do with my father's scheming and I believe I've now ensured you will no longer be troubled by him."

Merle was silent a long moment as he stared down at the braided rug, digesting Cody's words. Then with a resigned sigh, he lifted his gaze to Cody's. "You're a better man than I am."

Cody shook his head. "Maybe, maybe not. I've done things I'm not proud of, too, sir. None of us are without fault."

But he'd never cheat on a woman he claimed to love. He'd never cheat on Paris.

"I take full responsibility for my role in this." Shoulders slumped, Merle wearily raked his fingers through his hair. "There wouldn't have been an opportunity for your father to exploit had I been a man of honor. If I'd been the man my wife and daughter believed me to be—the kind of man you apparently are."

How long had Cody yearned for Paris's father to recognize that about him? That, although a child of poverty and the son of Leroy Hawk, he was a man worthy of respect. *God's man.* But he didn't feel an expected I-told-you-so triumph at the acknowledgment. He could only feel pity for Merle Perslow, a man who'd been given so much and thrown it all away.

Merle let out a pent-up breath. "You were right, weren't you, Cody, those many years ago?"

"Sir?"

"You told me one day I'd be groveling at your feet. And here I am." He hesitantly extended his hand. "Can you forgive me for judging you by the behaviors of your father and brothers? For making a cruel spectacle of you and your nephew at the Christmas gala?"

Could he?

Forgive us our trespasses as we forgive those who trespass against us. His business partner's father always said it was a waste of time and energy not to forgive—a disobedience toward God.

"I can, sir." He clasped the other man's hand. "I'm serious about testifying should that be the path you decide to take. My dad's in no shape to be hauled through the court system and there's no telling what finding out about this would do to Ma. But I realize there are consequences for wrong choices such as my dad's made."

"His wrong choices are no worse than mine." Merle picked up the envelope from the coffee table, opened the flap and gazed down at the contents.

"More harm than good would come from holding your father publicly accountable. I deserve the scandal, the disapproval and rejection by family and friends that would ensue. But Paris doesn't."

"No, sir, she doesn't."

Merle stepped to the fireplace and tossed the packet into the flames. It quickly caught fire, the corners curling and the contents soon consumed.

Their eyes met in mutual understanding, then Merle shook his head as if trying to clear it of cobwebs. "I don't deserve this. Being absolved. Forgiven for the way I've treated you since you were a boy."

"None of us *deserves* forgiveness, Mr. Perslow. Isn't that what Christmas is all about? The coming of the One who paid the price to make forgiveness, the restoration of our relationship with Him and others, possible?"

"Indeed it is. But it will take me some time to come to terms with the gift you've given me. My actions have haunted me for fifteen long years."

"Fifteen years?" A small, stricken voice whispered from the open doorway. "You didn't tell me *you* were married when you confessed to having had an affair."

Her father blanched as he swung around to where Paris stood. He took a halting step toward her, his hand outstretched.

"Sweetheart, I—"

An icy cold flooded her body as she instinctively stepped back, staring at her father as if at a stranger. "You cheated on Mom? That's why Leroy Hawk blackmailed you?"

"I—"

"Who was this woman?" She fought for breath, fought back the sensation that she was falling, tumbling into a deep, dark abyss. "Please don't tell me it was Mom's best friend."

Dad's eyes widened as he held up his hands in denial. "No, no, not Elizabeth. A woman who lived here only a short time. Neither you nor your mother knew her."

She turned to Cody, her eyes appealing for confirmation. He'd no doubt looked at the pictures Dad had thrown into the fire and knew the truth.

He shook his head. "It wasn't Elizabeth. No one I recognized."

She momentarily squeezed her eyes shut, fighting back tears of relief.

"Honey, I'm sorry." Her father motioned feebly. "Not a day goes by that I don't wish I could go back in time and change things."

"But how could you do that to Mom, Dad? How?" She fisted her fingers, her voice barely above a whisper. "And how dare you lie to me and imply that it was only the *woman* in your little affair who was married?"

"I have no excuses. None. Except that I'd do anything within my power to keep from hurting you."

A tiny whimper escaped Paris's lips. "Maybe you should have thought of that fifteen years ago. After what you confessed to me, I thought... I consoled myself that in your grief over Mom's death, in your loneliness, you made a mistake. But that's not what happened is it?"

"I did make a mistake. The worst mistake of my entire life." He looked to Cody, as if appealing for support. "Her mother's prolonged illness, watching her suffer, had worn me down and I selfishly reached out to another for comfort. But things went too far."

Paris pressed her hand momentarily to her mouth as a horrifying possibility leaped into her mind. "Mom...never knew, did she?"

"No, honey. No. I cut off the relationship after only a few weeks, so ashamed of what I'd done. But Leroy stumbled on us, used it against me. I went along with his demands to protect your mother. To protect you."

"And yourself."

"Yes." He bowed his head. "And myself."

"I don't know how I can ever—" Fearful of saying something she might forever regret, she spun away from him and ran from the room. But she'd just reached the foyer staircase when a firm grip on her arm drew her to a halt.

But it wasn't Dad. It was Cody, his distressed gaze capturing hers as he turned her toward him.

She struggled to free herself. "Let go of me."

"Paris. Calm down. Listen to me."

"I don't want to listen to you. I don't want to listen to any of you *lying* men."

His brow creased. "I've never lied to you."

"Oh, really?" She stared at him in disbelief. "A sin of omission is just as black as one of commission."

Confusion flickered in his eyes. "What do you mean?"

"How long have you known about my father's infidelity? How long were you going to keep silent?" She glared at the hands that held her captive. "And I said let go of me."

"Now, Paris—"

But he released her and she stepped back. "You found out last week, didn't you? I knew something was wrong. Why didn't you tell me? I've been worried sick that you were having second thoughts about us. Then you didn't return my calls. Accept my apology. So I was left to believe the worst, that Dad was right about you."

"I'm sorry, Paris. I didn't know what to do. I'd just pried everything out of my dad and was still trying to confirm the truth of it. Then when I did, when I found the evidence being used against your dad, I didn't think it was mine to tell."

He reached for her hand, but she pulled it away. "And just who else could I trust to tell me? Dad?"

"I knew it would hurt you, cause a rift in your relationship with your father."

"So were you *never* going to tell me?" At the guilty flicker in his eyes she turned away, but his hand on her arm stayed her and she reluctantly faced him again.

"Look, I'm sorry. I was wrong." His anguish-filled eyes met hers, imploring for understanding. "And I'm sorry for the way I left you at the Christmas gala. I wasn't thinking straight. I saw Deron up there on the stage and I overreacted."

"That was Dad's doing. Not mine."

"I know that now."

"I don't think I can ever forgive him for doing that to you and Deron, for how he implicated you in blackmail." She blinked back tears. "Or for what he did to Mom."

"I know it doesn't seem possible right now." Cody stared down at her, his eyes filled with understanding. "But you can. And you will. But it will take time."

She pressed her lips together, trying to still their trembling, hold back the tears. "I can't bear to speak to him. To see him. I don't want to spend another night under the same roof with him."

"I understand…but I think he needs you right now."

She stared. "You're siding with him?"

"I don't condone what he did, Paris. I thought the world of your mother. I'm angry with your dad and my dad. I'm just saying that fifteen years ago he made a mistake. A bad, bad mistake he's had to live with for a decade and a half. He's suffering."

"And I'm not?"

"That's not what I'm saying."

She impulsively reached for his hand, her eyes beseeching. "Then let's leave town tonight, Cody. Together."

Cody's breath caught. She still wanted him in her life even after learning of the role Leroy Hawk played in blackmailing her father? But there were other issues less easily resolved.

"I don't think that's such a good idea, Paris."

She squeezed his hand. "Why not? I'm not suggesting we do anything immoral, something we'd come to regret. I told you I planned to leave after the first of the year for a fresh start, remember?"

"Yes, but—"

"I can go back to school or get a job. Maybe get an apartment in the same complex as yours. Unless…" She tilted her head to look up at him with hope-filled eyes. "Unless you're ready to make things permanent."

He swallowed. "Permanent?"

"You know…?" She gazed shyly up at him, a blush tingeing her cheeks.

"Oh."

But, judging from the dismay in her eyes, that was an inadequate response to a woman who had marriage on her mind. To a woman who'd been led to believe that was his intent, as well. A weight settled into Cody's chest. How could he make her understand, yet not hurt her?

He took her other hand in his as well, his words measured. "I'm not sure making it…us…permanent is a good idea."

Apprehension flickered through her eyes, but she quickly rallied. "Why not? Dad can hardly object to you now, can he? I overheard enough of the conversation between the two of you to know he owes you. Even he recognized it and admitted he was wrong about you."

"The fact of the matter, though, is…" He was still the son of Leroy Hawk. Son of an alcoholic, an extortionist and a liar extraordinaire. A half brother to two men who had a rap sheet a mile long. People around here wouldn't be likely to forget that. And why should they when he couldn't?

"The fact of the matter," she prodded, tension evident in her tone, "is what?"

He ran his thumbs gently across the back of her hands. "As much as we'd like to ignore it, pretend it doesn't exist and won't have a lasting effect on us, we still come from vastly different worlds, Paris."

He'd given it a lot of thought and prayer these past few days. Yeah, he was a different man today than the angry, callow youth who'd left town a dozen years ago. But he still had a lot of growing up to do. Spiritually. Professionally. Paris deserved so much more than he could ever offer her.

"What are you saying?"

"I'm saying…we need to step back. Allow ourselves some breathing room."

She swallowed. "Breathing room."

"We both have a lot on our plates right now. You—your Dad's situation and working through that. Figuring out what you want to do with your future. And me—Ma, Dad, Deron and getting my business off the ground. Well, it's a lot, you know?"

"I see."

But she didn't. He could tell by the injured look in her eyes that she didn't recognize that even though it was killing him to say these things, he had to. For her own good. He couldn't bear to tear her away from a privileged life in Canyon Springs, tear her from her family and friends and all that was familiar. To ask her to journey by his side to a destination he couldn't yet see on the horizon and had no idea how it would all work out.

What if the business deal backfired and he lost everything he'd worked for? What if no one in this town could see beyond his past and, as Paris's father had long insinuated, his involvement with her tainted her reputation, her happiness, for a lifetime?

No, that might not be faith-filled thinking, but he had to weigh the possibilities, face reality.

"I'm sorry, Paris, I'd really hoped—"

She pulled her hands from his. Tears pooled in her eyes as she looked up at him, a disbelieving laugh escaping her lips. "You had me convinced you didn't trust me. That you were afraid I'd head for the hills at the first sign of opposition and break your heart. But it turns out *you're* the one who can't be trusted, Cody Hawk."

Before he could react, she dashed up the stairs, leaving him to stand staring after her.

Chapter Twenty-Three

Paris made her way slowly down the aisle with the throng of Christmas Eve churchgoers exiting the service. From her seat near the front of the church—Dad insisted she sit with him—she hadn't seen Cody tonight. Had he gone back to Phoenix, back to the world he'd lived in apart from her these past twelve years?

She said a silent prayer for him. For them. But there was no *them*. He'd made that clear.

Light snow had continued to fall all day, lending Bill and Sharon's afternoon wedding a season-suitable glow. But Paris had found it difficult to keep her mind on the touching ceremony.

"Sweetheart," Dad whispered as they moved down the aisle. "I'm going to Elizabeth's after this. Will you be coming?"

The Herrington and Perslow clans had shared a longtime Christmas Eve tradition of cocoa and cookies after the service. She only wanted to go home, but because Elizabeth had confessed her role in Dalton's return to town, she knew she should put in an appearance. Despite her own confession of guilt and their tears shed together, she wouldn't want Elizabeth to misconstrue that she held her to blame.

Paris gave a little sigh. She hadn't had a chance to tell Cody about that twist in events…how, because of her own long-held perception of responsibility for Dalton's death, she'd been able to comfort his equally guilt-ridden mother.

"Paris?" Dad touched her arm.

"Oh, sorry. I'll stop by for a little while. I'm pretty tired."

"No word from Cody, I take it?"

She shook her head.

"He cares for you, Paris. He has for a long time. He'll be back." Her father clearly wanted to say more, but they were still on shaky ground in their own relationship. He'd apologized repeatedly, not only for his unfaithfulness but for his misconceptions of Cody. For playing a role in keeping them apart.

She loved her father and had forgiven him as a matter of the will alone, a decision in obedience to God's expectation. But her feelings on the matter of his betrayal of her mother still clamored.

She now better understood, though, why Dad remained unmarried after Mom died. Just as she played a lonely, blame-filled role following Dalton's death, Dad had done likewise even after the passing of Elizabeth's husband. He'd no doubt feared that she, a woman Paris suspected he much admired, might somehow also become implicated in Leroy's schemes. And what man wanted to confess a past infidelity to a woman he wished to woo?

Her dad kissed her on the forehead. "I'm going to slip out the back way. I'll see you in a bit."

He departed and, heart heavy, Paris slowly made her way to the front foyer. She smiled and murmured responses to greetings of the season, noting with longing the many parents with sleeping infants in their arms and youngsters eager to get home "with visions of sugarplums" dancing in their heads.

At the door, Pastor Kenton took her hand. "Reyna and I can't thank you enough for handling the three weddings."

"I'm glad I was able to help."

He wiggled his brows. "I don't suppose you'd be interested in taking on the lead wedding coordinator role again?"

Was she? No. She'd proven to herself and her family and friends that she could do it. With God's and Cody's help, she'd begun to move beyond the tragedy.

"I'm afraid not, Jason. Besides, I think Reyna missed not being in the thick of things these past few weeks. She's a born romantic, if you hadn't noticed."

"Indeed I have. But thank you. And Merry Christmas, Paris."

She headed to her SUV in the far corner of the parking lot, the snow falling around her and crunching under her booted feet. The cries of holiday wishes from those departing the church rang hollowly in her ears.

Merry Christmas. Happy holidays.

She flipped the lock switch on the key in her hand and her vehicle momentarily lit up under a light layer of snow.

"Excuse me, miss," a male voice came from behind her, "but could you use help cleaning off your car?"

Heart racing, she turned slowly to Cody. Tall, handsome, with fluffy snowflakes lighting in his hair, he held up his trusty heavy-duty snowbrush.

She watched in silence as he effortlessly swept the inch-deep layer from her windows, the hood and the roof. Then he turned to her once again, his gaze as uncertain as she felt.

"So you didn't leave town after all," Paris ventured. "I thought maybe you had."

"Actually, I just got back from Phoenix. I didn't want to miss out on Christmas with Ma and Deron."

Of course he'd return for that. For them.

"So Santa has things covered?" He'd told her that day outside Camilla's that he'd be calling on her for assistance. He hadn't.

He squared his shoulders. "I think the jolly old elf has done all right for himself."

She offered a smile. "Good."

How delightful it would be to watch the little boy tear into his packages tomorrow morning, to see Cody and his mother joining in on the fun. But she and Dad would go to her paternal grandparents' house—her mother's parents were still on a month-long cruise—then on a round of afternoon holiday open houses.

Cody shifted his weight, his gaze again catching hers. "How are…things going with your dad?"

"It's awkward. We're handling each other with kid gloves. He's brokenhearted, ashamed. Yet I sense there's a relief there now that he's not bearing the burden alone, that he's accepting forgiveness." She took a quick breath. "But I still can't believe he did what he did. I love my dad and I've chosen to forgive him just as I know Mom would have. But I'm still struggling to come to terms with it."

"Give yourself time. This was a severe blow."

"I know, but it feels as if the foundation of my whole world has collapsed."

"But you know it didn't," Cody said softly, his eyes filled with compassion. "Jesus is your foundation, Paris, not your dad. You can stand firm on His promises."

She nodded. "I keep reminding myself of that."

He placed the snowbrush on top of her SUV and thrust his hands into his jacket pockets. "I'm reminding myself of those promises, too."

She tilted her head. "In what way?"

He scuffed a booted toe in the snow, a faint smile

surfacing. "In case you never noticed, even after all those years living outside of Canyon Springs and giving myself to God, I still managed to return to town with a mountain-size chip on my shoulder."

"What? You?" She gave a little laugh. "Oh, surely not."

His smile broadened. "Go ahead. Make fun."

"Me? Never."

He shook his head, the momentary brightness in his eyes dimming. "I guess what I'm trying to say is that I have a lot of pride issues."

Memory flashed to the day he'd refused the gift cards intended for his mother. How he'd snatched Deron from the stage.

"Pride issues can get out of hand," he continued, his gaze riveted on her. "Issues I've used to justify holding people at arm's length and refusing to believe the best in them. Issues to defend keeping old wounds alive and rationalizing not trusting God... in matters of the heart."

A flicker of hope sparked.

"You've had a lot to overcome, Cody."

"That's no excuse." He took a step closer. "Not when pride and a bad attitude keep me from accepting the love of a woman I've long believed God made for me. And me for her."

Paris's throat went suddenly dry.

"I've made plenty of mistakes in my life", he continued. "Quite a few since returning to Canyon Springs. I know I've hurt you. Disappointed you.

But no matter how you might feel about me now, I love you, Paris. I've always loved you and I'll forever love you."

A dizzying sensation raced through her. She'd thought when she'd turned her back on him and ran up the stairs, that she'd never see him again. And, yet, here he was, saying all the things she'd so desperately prayed she'd one day hear.

"I love you, too, Cody."

He reached out to cup her face in his surprisingly warm, bare hands. "Can you forgive me for being slow to become the man you need me to be? To be the man God wants me to be for you?"

She nodded. "I can and I do. But will you forgive me for not recognizing you were the man of my dreams twelve years ago? For not standing up to my father even when deep in my heart I knew the truth?"

"Done deal." His eyes smiled into hers. "But new rule, Paris. No regrets. That's all in our past, a past God used to bring us to who and where we are today."

She placed her hand over Cody's, her eyes never leaving his. "Is this where I'm supposed to beg you to marry me?"

"Mmm." He hemmed and hawed, pretending to consider, then grinned. "I might enjoy hearing that. But you know, I think I can take it from here."

To her astonishment, he dropped to one knee in

the snow, reaching into his jacket pocket to produce a small, ornament-shaped box. Paris gasped as he opened it to reveal a diamond ring sparkling in the dim, snowy light.

He extracted it and took her hand, his gaze holding hers captive. "I don't know whether this is premature or twelve years late…but will you marry me, Paris Perslow?"

Breathless, she stared into his love-filled eyes.

"To have and to hold from this day forward," he prompted. "And all that other good stuff?"

She couldn't contain her smile. "I like the sound of that.'"

"That's a yes?"

"It is."

He slipped the ring on her finger, then she drew him back to his feet where they stood entwined in each other's arms as snowflakes danced in the dark around them.

He gently leaned his forehead against hers. "If God would have told me four weeks ago that by Christmas I'd be engaged to marry you, I never would have believed Him."

She pulled back slightly and brushed the snow from his dark hair, a coquettish smile forming on her lips. "Would you have believed Him if He told you you'd not only have a fiancée by Christmas, but you'd be kissing her, too?"

He cocked a brow. "Is that a hint?"

"I think…it is."

"Then Merry Christmas, Paris." Eyes dancing, he gathered her more closely in his arms and touched his lips to hers.

Epilogue

Noisemakers sounded and confetti flew in the great room of the Perslows' home as Cody grabbed Paris's hand and pulled her aside for a kiss.

Paris. His love. His soon-to-be bride.

Thank you, God.

"Happy New Year, Paris," he said softly.

"Happy New Year, Cody." Her eyes smiled into his. "I still wake up each morning, wondering if this is a dream."

"Believe me, it's real." Cody leaned in again, certain another kiss would convince her, but her father laughingly tugged at his arm. "Come on, you two, there's plenty of time later for such as that. Let's have a toast."

With a regretful look at Paris, Cody handed her a punch glass, then lifted his as the other guests did the same.

"Thank you for joining me tonight." Merle beamed a smile around the room that made him look years younger than when Cody had first met with him only a few days after Thanksgiving. Was that what forgiveness did? Or the added fact that Elizabeth Herrington smiled at him with a special sparkle in her eyes?

"I want to take this opportunity to thank God for His many blessings," Merle continued, "and most of all for the gift of His son, Jesus Christ."

Several guests clapped.

"We all—I'm including myself here—daily fall short of the expectations God has for us. We miss the mark, sometimes by a long shot. But He loves us anyway." Merle shook his head as if in wonder. "I, for one, am humbly grateful for that gift."

"Amen," someone murmured.

"And now…I wish to all of you the happiest of new years." Merle lifted his punch glass, then turned to Paris and Cody. "And especially to my daughter and soon-to-be new son."

Cody's gaze met Merle's and he nodded an acknowledgment as Paris hurried over to give her dad a hug. Yes, a lot of healing remained to be done in all their lives and it would take time. Patience. Trust. But undoubtedly, God had been at work and would continue to work in them.

Following a round of renewed congratulations at their engagement, Cody led Paris to the front foyer where he snagged her teddy-bear coat off a wall peg and helped her into it. Together they slipped out onto the porch, into the chill, snow-filled night.

At the railing he stepped in behind her, wrapped his arms around her and pulled her close. For several silent minutes, they watched snow gently descend, settling on the ponderosa pine branches as fairy lights strung through the trees lent a surreal glow to their surroundings.

Cody could feel God smiling on them.

He gave his fiancée a hug. "I've loved you, Paris Perslow, since the day I first laid eyes on you."

"And you've always been my hero." She snuggled closer. "Yet it's only been in the past month that God turned over the tangled thread side of the tapestry of our lives so we can see the beauty of the pattern He's been working on."

He leaned his head against her silky hair. "Waxing poetic tonight, are you?"

"I always wax poetic when I'm around you. Someday I'll show you the poems I wrote when I was a teenager. You drew pictures of me and I wrote poetry about you."

Cody drew back. "You're kidding."

"No."

"I showed you one of my sketches, why didn't you show me your poetry?"

"Get real." She turned in his arms to face him, a teasing smile on her lips. "I was determined to squelch those stirrings of what I'd begun to feel for you. I was terrified Dad would find out, too."

"He seems good with it now. With me. Us." He

frowned. "Or do you think it's an act because he doesn't want to lose you?"

She lifted her chin. "No, Dad's for real. God's opened his eyes to many things in recent weeks. When he called you son, he meant it."

"If only my own dad's eyes would be opened before it's too late." It didn't appear as if Leroy Hawk would be long for this world.

"Never forget that with God there's *always* hope."

"There is." His heart lightened at the assurance in her voice, and his thoughts turned to the future. Their future. "I'm happy you feel the same way I do about renting a weekend cabin up here until we can, hopefully, relocate somewhere in mountain country."

He and Trevor saw real possibilities up here in the number of second homes thrown on the market during the recession. He'd be better able to cover the territory without such a long commute.

"And I'm all for taking Deron in if your brother and Deron's mother don't refuse us. But I have a strong feeling right here—" she pressed her hand to her heart "—that they'll be more than willing to let him go."

"Then he'll be our first kid."

"He will."

"You're going to fit right into his life, Paris. You're already fitting into Ma's. She loved the scarf and gloves and—" he cast her an apologetic look "—the gift cards."

Paris gave a soft laugh, then pulled back to look up at him. "Now, wasn't there something my dad said right before his toast? You know, about something we'd have plenty of time for later?"

Cody cocked a brow, his gaze locking with hers. "That may have been in reference to…kissing."

"Ah, yes, I remember now." Paris tilted her head playfully. "It's later now, isn't it?"

"I do believe it is." He tightened his arms around her waist, his heartbeat stepping up a notch.

"Well, then, what are we waiting for?" Applying gentle pressure to the back of his neck, she drew his mouth down to hers.

* * * * *

Dear Reader,

I've long looked forward to writing a Christmas story set in fictional Canyon Springs! The mountain country of Arizona is so beautiful during this special time of year, with snowflakes dancing in the air and the towering ponderosa pines flocked with snow-fog. Hot chocolate topped with whipped cream and cinnamon, peppermint candy canes and orange-flavored white chocolate are all favorites to enjoy while I cozy in to reread the Biblical passages of the first Christmas.

Cody and Paris's love story has served as a good reminder to me of what this season is all about—celebrating the coming of the One who paid the price to make true forgiveness, the restoration of our relationship with God and others, available. Both Paris and Cody must overcome their pasts to accept themselves and love each other. They must learn to receive and extend forgiveness to others even when, amidst the outcries of their wounded hearts, it might seem impossible. But God, through the arrival of His long-awaited Son, makes it possible.

I pray that during this Christmas season and the coming year you will pause to reflect on and thankfully embrace this very special Gift.

Wishing you the many blessings of this season…
Glynna Kaye

Questions for Discussion

1. Paris approaches the holiday season knowing that in the coming year she needs to make a change. Have you ever had a time in your life that you sensed God nudging you out of your comfort zone? Did you take those guided steps? What happened?

2. Paris has carried a burden of guilt over Dalton's death for years. How did this affect her relationship with Cody and others? Is there anything in your own life you need to accept God's forgiveness for—and forgive yourself for?

3. Cody has been, as he thinks of it, "stuffed in a box of preconceptions." Have you ever had a similar experience? How did it affect the way you faced life?

4. Because of past events, Paris initially distrusts her growing attraction to Cody. She loves and respects her father, so what leads her to go against his wishes and allow herself to care for Cody? Was this a wise move?

5. Paris cares deeply for those she loves, but fell into a long-term pattern of people-pleasing and

going along with whatever others felt her life should be. How might she live a better-balanced life in the future?

6. Cody's heart is set against anything he interprets as a "handout." Can you identify with his feelings? How might he be taking those feelings too far and taking offense where none was intended? How do you see him dealing with these feelings in the future?

7. Cody returned to town with expectations that his father would apologize for the way he'd treated Cody. Do you think Cody is right that extending forgiveness can be as much for the one who's been wronged as for the one who did the wrong? Is there someone in your own life who may *never* ask for forgiveness but who needs to be forgiven so *you* can receive God's peace?

8. Why do you think Cody so strongly identifies with Deron? How does this identification drive Cody's behavior? In Deron's future do you foresee a parallel to Cody's relationship with his "adopted" father?

9. Regardless of their love for each other, Paris and Cody *do* come from vastly different back-

grounds. How do you think these differences will impact their future together? What reactions from the community, friends and extended family can Paris and Cody realistically expect?

10. If you were Paris and Cody, would you return to live in Canyon Springs—or move to another nearby mountain town? Why?

LARGER-PRINT BOOKS!

GET 2 FREE LARGER-PRINT NOVELS PLUS 2 FREE MYSTERY GIFTS

Love Inspired®
SUSPENSE
RIVETING INSPIRATIONAL ROMANCE

Larger-print novels are now available...

YES! Please send me 2 FREE LARGER-PRINT Love Inspired® Suspense novels and my 2 FREE mystery gifts (gifts are worth about $10). After receiving them, if I don't wish to receive any more books, I can return the shipping statement marked "cancel." If I don't cancel, I will receive 4 brand-new novels every month and be billed just $5.24 per book in the U.S. or $5.74 per book in Canada. That's a savings of at least 23% off the cover price. It's quite a bargain! Shipping and handling is just 50¢ per book in the U.S. and 75¢ per book in Canada.* I understand that accepting the 2 free books and gifts places me under no obligation to buy anything. I can always return a shipment and cancel at any time. Even if I never buy another book, the two free books and gifts are mine to keep forever.

110/310 IDN F5CC

Name	(PLEASE PRINT)	
Address		Apt. #
City	State/Prov.	Zip/Postal Code

Signature (if under 18, a parent or guardian must sign)

Mail to the Harlequin® Reader Service:
IN U.S.A.: P.O. Box 1867, Buffalo, NY 14240-1867
IN CANADA: P.O. Box 609, Fort Erie, Ontario L2A 5X3

Are you a current subscriber to Love Inspired Suspense books and want to receive the larger-print edition?
Call 1-800-873-8635 or visit www.ReaderService.com.

* Terms and prices subject to change without notice. Prices do not include applicable taxes. Sales tax applicable in N.Y. Canadian residents will be charged applicable taxes. Offer not valid in Quebec. This offer is limited to one order per household. Not valid for current subscribers to Love Inspired Suspense larger-print books. All orders subject to credit approval. Credit or debit balances in a customer's account(s) may be offset by any other outstanding balance owed by or to the customer. Please allow 4 to 6 weeks for delivery. Offer available while quantities last.

Your Privacy—The Harlequin® Reader Service is committed to protecting your privacy. Our Privacy Policy is available online at www.ReaderService.com or upon request from the Harlequin Reader Service.

We make a portion of our mailing list available to reputable third parties that offer products we believe may interest you. If you prefer that we not exchange your name with third parties, or if you wish to clarify or modify your communication preferences, please visit us at www.ReaderService.com/consumerschoice or write to us at Harlequin Reader Service Preference Service, P.O. Box 9062, Buffalo, NY 14269. Include your complete name and address.

LISLPDIR13R

ReaderService.com

Manage your account online!

- Review your order history
- Manage your payments
- Update your address

---

*We've designed
the Harlequin® Reader Service
website just for you.*

Enjoy all the features!

- Reader excerpts from any series
- Respond to mailings and special monthly offers
- Discover new series available to you
- Browse the Bonus Bucks catalog
- Share your feedback

Visit us at:

ReaderService.com